# HOLIDAY IN A COMA

*and*

# LOVE LASTS THREE YEARS

Also by Frédéric Beigbeder

*Windows on the World*

FRÉDÉRIC BEIGBEDER

# HOLIDAY IN A COMA

*and*

# LOVE LASTS THREE YEARS

*Two Novels*

TRANSLATED FROM THE FRENCH BY
FRANK WYNNE

FOURTH ESTATE • *London*

First published in Great Britain in 2007 by
Fourth Estate
An imprint of HarperCollins*Publishers*
77–85 Fulham Palace Road
London W6 8JB
www.4thestate.co.uk

1

A catalogue record for this book is available from the British Library

ISBN 978-0-00-722813-3

Typeset in Minion by Palimpsest Book Production Limited,
Grangemouth, Stirlingshire

Printed in Great Britain by Clays Ltd, St Ives plc

This book is proudly printed on paper which contains wood
from well managed forests, certified in accordance with
the rules of the Forest Stewardship Council.
For more information about FSC,
please visit www.fsc-uk.org

# HOLIDAY IN A COMA

*For Diane B.,*
*I fell,*
*Head over heels.*

Let's dance
The last dance
Tonight
Yes it's my last chance
For romance
Tonight.

Donna Summer, 'Last Dance'
Casablanca Records

Second novels are written in a secondary
frame of mind.

Me

# 7.00 P.M.

He combs his hair, puts on or takes off his
jacket or his scarf as one might toss a flower
into a grave which is still open'

Jean-Jacques Schuhl
*Rose Poussière*

Marc Marronnier is twenty-seven years old, he has a beautiful apartment, a cool job and still he doesn't kill himself. Go figure.

His doorbell rings. Marc Marronnier loves a lot of things: the photos in the American edition of *Harper's Bazaar*, Irish whiskey straight up, the avenue Vélasquez, a song ('God Only Knows' by the Beach Boys), chocolate éclairs, a book (*les Deux Veuves* by Dominique Noguez) and belated ejaculation. Doorbells ringing is not one of those things.

'Monsieur Marronnier?' asks a bell-boy in a motorcycle helmet.

'In the flesh.'

'This is for you.'

The bell-boy in the motorcycle helmet (he looks like 'Spirou and the Golden Bowl') hands him an envelope approximately three feet square, jiggling impatiently as though he urgently needs a piss. Marc takes the envelope and gives him a ten-franc piece to disappear out of his life. Marc Marronnier doesn't need a bell-boy in a motorcycle helmet in his life.

Inside the envelope, he is utterly unsurprised to discover the following:

# A NIGHT IN SHIT

\* \* \* \* \* \* \* \* \*

Grand Opening Night
Place de la Madeleine
Paris

He is, however, pretty surprised to find, stapled to the invitation:

*See you tonight, you old queer*
*Joss Dumoulin*
*DJ*

JOSS DUMOULIN? Marc was sure he was living in permanent exile in Japan. Or dead.

But dead men don't host club nights.

And so Marc Marronnier brushes his fingers through his hair, a gesture that indicates a certain inner contentment. It has to be said, he's been waiting a long time for 'a night in Shit'. Every day for the past year he's walked past the construction site for the new club, 'the biggest nightclub in Paris'. And every time he passes, he thinks, on opening night, there are going to be a truckload of honeys.

Marc Marronnier aims to please. This is probably why he wears glasses. When they're perched on his nose, his colleagues think he looks like William Hurt, only uglier. (NB His myopia dates from his secondary school days at Louis-le-Grand, his scoliosis from his days studying at Sciences Po.)

It's official: Marc Marronnier is going to have sexual relations tonight, whatever happens. He may even do the deed with more than one person, who knows? He has packed six condoms, for he is an ambitious young man.

10

Marc Marronnier senses he is going to die, in forty years or so. When he's quite finished getting on our nerves.

Society scoundrel, armchair rebel, photo-opportunity mercenary, disgraceful bourgeois, his life consists of listening to messages on his answering machine and leaving them on other answering machines. All the while watching thirty channels simultaneously using picture-in-picture on cable TV. He sometimes forgets to eat for several days.

On the day he was born, he was already a has-been. There are countries where one dies at a ripe old age, in Neuilly-sur-Seine, you are born at an old age. Blasé before he had lived a day, he now cultivates his failures. For example, he boasts about writing slim volumes of barely a hundred pages with print runs of less than 3,000. 'Since literature is dead, I make do with writing for my friends,' he eructates at formal dinners, knocking back the dregs from the glasses of the girls sitting next to him. It is important that Neuilly-sur-Seine not give up hope.

A nightlife correspondent, copywriter–editor, literary journalist: Marc cannot commit to anything. He refuses to choose one life over another. These days, he says, 'everyone is insane, the only choice left is between schizophrenia and paranoia: we are either many in one or one against all'. And yet, like all chameleons (Fregoli, Zelig, Thierry Le Luron), if there is one thing he hates, it is being alone. This is why there are multiple Marc Marronniers.

Delphine Seyrig passed away in the late morning, it is now 7 p.m. Marc has taken off his glasses to brush his teeth. I've just told you he is unstable by nature.

Is Marc Marronnier happy? Well, he's got nothing to complain about. He spends vast sums of money every month and has no children. That, surely, is happiness: having no problems. And yet, from time to time he feels something like worry in his belly. The annoying thing is that he is unable to determine what kind of worry. It is an Unidentified Anguish. It makes him cry watching dreadful movies. He is definitely missing something, but what? Thank God the feeling invariably wears off.

In the meantime, it will be very strange for him to see Joss Dumoulin again after all this time. Joss Dumoulin, dubbed 'the million dollar DJ' in last month's *Vanity Fair*: an old friend who hit the big time. Marc is unsure if he is really happy about the fact that Joss has become so famous. He feels like a sprinter still at the starting-blocks, watching his best mate ascend the podium to howls of adulation from the crowd.

In a nutshell, Joss Dumoulin is master of the universe, since he practises the most important profession in the world in the greatest city in the world: he is the best DJ in Tokyo.

Is it really necessary to remind you how the DJs seized power? In a hedonistic society as superficial as ours, the citizens of the world are interested in only one thing: partying. (Sex and money being implicitly part and parcel of the whole: money facilitates partying which facilitates sex.) And DJs have complete control. Not content just with clubs, they spawn the rave culture and have people dancing in warehouses, car parks, building sites, any available patch of waste ground. They are the ones who killed off rock and roll, inventing first rap and then house. They lord it over the Top 40 by day and the clubs by night. It's getting hard to avoid them.

DJs remix our lives. Nobody gives them a hard time about it: if you're going to hand over power to someone, a DJ is at least as qualified as a movie star or an ex-lawyer. After all, to govern, all you need is a good ear, a little general knowledge and the ability to segue.

Being a DJ is a curious profession. Somewhere between priest and prostitute. You give everything you have to people who give nothing in return. You spin discs so that other people can dance, have it large, come on to the pretty girl in the skin-tight dress. Then you head home on your own with your records under your arm. Being a DJ is a dilemma. A DJ exists only through other people: he steals other people's music to get other people to dance. He's a mix of Robin Hood (steals from one to give to the other) and Cyrano de Bergerac (living his life by proxy). All in all, the most important profession of our time is enough to drive anyone mad.

Joss Dumoulin didn't squander his youth at the Institut d'Études Politiques like Marc. At twenty, he headed straight for Japan with nothing in his luggage except the three Bs of success: Bone Idleness, Bullshit Artistry and Bigging It Up. Why Japan? Because, he used to say, 'If you're going to take a gap year somewhere, you might as well head for the richest country on earth. It's all about the Benjamins, baby.'

Of course, Joss's gap year turned into a gap life. In no time flat he was the mascot of Nippon nightlife. His club nights at Juliana's, it is said, were bangin'. It has to be said he arrived at just the right time: Tokyo was just discovering the delights of capitalist decadence. Government ministers were increasingly corrupt, foreigners increasingly numerous. Tokyo's gilded youth was having a hard time spending all their parents' money. All in all, Marc Marronnier took the wrong turn.

He went over for a visit once. He can confirm that Joss Dumoulin has only to walk into Gold and suddenly every guy in the place is snorting loudly or popping little bits of blotter. As for the girls, they turn themselves into geishas as he walks by. Marc has Polaroids in a drawer somewhere to prove it.

Joss Dumoulin has lived Marc Marronnier's life for him. Pulled all the girls he doesn't have the balls to talk to. Taken all the drugs he's afraid to try. Joss is the polar opposite of Marc; maybe this is why they got on so well once upon a time.

Marc only drinks fizzy drinks: Coca-Cola in the morning, Berocca in the afternoon, vodka and tonic at night. He fills himself with bubbles all day long. As he puts down his glass of Alka-Seltzer (just this once), he thinks back to Tokyo bay and that fantastically Pacific ocean.

He remembers the night he spent at Love and Sex on the top floor of Gold where a dozen of Joss's mates fucked some Chink girl as innocent as she was handcuffed. It was here, after he'd had his turn, that Marc was introduced to Joss's wife. You learn something new every night.

Marc is horribly unlucky: his parents are in great shape. Every day, they fritter away a little more of his inheritance. Meanwhile, the Digital Sampler, a machine invented in the mid-eighties, has made Joss Dumoulin rich and famous. The sampler makes it possible to nick the best bits from any piece of music and recycle them to make 'dance' tracks. Thanks to this invention, DJs, who were previously little more than human jukeboxes, have become musicians in their own right. (It's as if librarians were writing books or museum curators painting pictures.) Joss was quick on the uptake: suddenly, his productions flooded the Japanese club market and from there the world. All he need do is drag out whatever he likes from his record collection and serve it up to his nocturnal public. He watches their reactions, ditches anything that doesn't make them dance, notes what works. He feels his way: there is no better focus group than a dance floor. This is how you become an inter-national star while your old friend goes on uselessly studying.

Commercial success wasn't long in coming. It was Joss who first mixed birdsong with Mesopotamian choirs: the record was number one in thirty countries including Sri Lanka and the Commonwealth of Independent States. Then Joss launched bossa-soukouss over a melody stolen from the Goldberg Variations: a huge hit which made it onto the heavy rotation playlist of MTV Europe. Marc still laughs when he thinks about that summer when, thanks to Dumoulin's bossa-soukouss video (sponsored by Orangina), everyone was doing the dance where you yank the girl's breasts.

And so on and so on: Joss chalked up a fortune pretty quickly. Georges Guétary dressed in Jean-Paul Gaultier singing traditional Israeli chants? Joss produced that one: twenty-three weeks at number one in the French charts. Techno-gospel? Joss. That instrumental with Archie Shepp playing sax over a drum solo by Keith Moon (of course you remember – the one that made acid jazz seem gay)? That was Joss. The Sylvie Vartan–Johnny Rotten duet? Joss again. Right now (Marc read about it in the *Vanity Fair* article where Joss was photographed by Annie Leibovitz drowning in a sea of quarter-inch tape), he's working on a mix featuring an Airbus A320 crashing and Petula Clark singing 'Don't Sleep in the Subway', a garage version of the speeches of Maréchal Pétain and a one-off concert at Wembley Stadium featuring Luciano Pavarotti singing with AC/DC. He's got his work cut out for him. His kleptomaniac imagination knows no bounds, to say nothing of his CD sales. Joss Dumoulin understands the age in which he lives: he only makes collages.

And here he is, Joss Dumoulin organising the grand opening of Shit, the club all of Paris has been waiting for. It's hardly a revelation: Joss does one-nighters all over the world. And not just anywhere: at Club USA (New York), Pacha (Madrid), the Ministry of Sound (London), 90° (Berlin), the Baby'O (Acapulco), the Bash (Miami), the Roxy (Amsterdam), the Mau-Mau (Buenos Aires), Alien (Rome) and – obviously – Space (Ibiza). Different sets where the same people are squirming, depending on the season. Marc is a little bitter but decides to look on the bright side. After all, Joss will be able to introduce him to the prettiest girls at the gig. Or at least the one he doesn't want for himself.

Marc has access to a network of informants: PR sluts and certified star-fuckers. They phone him to tell him that Shit really was built in an old public toilet. They've built a giant toilet on the place de la Madeleine. A six-feet-high pink bog roll serves as an awning above the entrance. But the main attraction, the thing that will completely revolutionise clubbing in Paris, is that they've built a submersible circular dance floor in the shape of a toilet seat, equipped with a giant flush mechanism which plunges the dancers into a huge whirlpool at some unspecified point during the evening. Marc also learns that, to maintain the element of surprise, the guests for the opening were deliberately not sent their invitations until the day of the opening, at the last possible minute. He thinks that most of the interesting people will somehow manage to wriggle out of their multiple prior engagements.

*

Although tonight he is spoiled for choice. Marc's coffee table groans under the weight of possibilities: a performance at a gallery opening on the rue des Beaux-Arts (the painter is scheduled to cut off both hands at around 9 p.m.), a dinner at the Arc in honour of the half-brother of Lenny Kravitz's bassist's best friend, a fancy-dress ball in the old Renault factory at Issy-les-Moulineaux to launch a new perfume (Assembly Line by Chanel), a private concert by the hot new English band (The John Lennons) at La Cigale, a themed party at Denise's on the 'Heterosexual Lesbians as Leather Queens in Drag' and a rave at the Élysée Palace. In spite of everything, Marc knows that all over the city, the question of the moment is: 'Are you going to Shit tonight?' (The uninitiated who misunderstands risks betraying not only his ignorance but a personal incontinence problem.)

Marc poses in front of the bathroom mirror. Tonight he's going to kiss girls he hasn't been introduced to. He's going to sleep with people he's never met, people he hasn't previously had fifteen intimate dinners with.

He's impressing nobody, especially not himself. Deep down, he knows he wants the same thing all his friends want: to fall in love again.

He grabs a white shirt and a navy blue tie with white polka dots, he shaves quickly, douses himself with eau de toilette, howls in pain and leaves the flat. He refuses to panic.

He thinks: 'Mythify everything because everything is mythic. Things, places, dates, people are all potential legends, you just have to find the right myth. Everyone who lived in Paris in 1940 will eventually be a character in a Patrick Modiano novel. Anyone who set foot in a London pub in 1965 will have slept with Mick Jagger. When you get down to it, being a legend is easy: you just have to wait your turn. Carnaby Street, the Hamptons, Greenwich Village, le Lac d'Aiguebelette, the Faubourg Saint-Germain, Goa, Guéthary, le Paradou, Mustique, Phuket: it doesn't matter if you're bored shitless at the time, and twenty years from now you can brag that you were there. Time is a sacrament. Sick and tired of your life? Hang in there and you'll be a legend.' Walking gives Marc some peculiar ideas.

The toughest problem is managing to be mythic and alive *at the same time.* Joss Dumoulin might have pulled it off.

Does a living legend keep his hands in his pockets? Does he wear a cashmere scarf? Does he agree to spend 'a night at Shit'?

Marc checks to make sure he has no signal on his mobile. No, not a single bar. There's no need to worry, then. It's perfectly normal that his phone isn't ringing. Marc will be uncontactable for another six yards.

There was a time when he went out every night, and not just for professional reasons. Sometimes he'd run into a certain Jocelyn du Moulin (oh yes, that's what he was called back in the day; the 'du' which indicates he's part of the old French aristocracy is something he only dropped recently: now he's pseudo-working class).

The weather is fine so Marc starts singing 'Singing in the Rain'. It's still better than humming 'Le Lundi au Soleil' when it's raining (especially given that it's Friday.)

Paris is a film set mock-up. Marc Marronnier wishes that it was all *really* made of pasteboard. He prefers the fake Pont Neuf, the one Leos Carax had built in the middle of nowhere, to the

18

real one that Christo wrapped. He wishes that this whole city were deliberately fake instead of pretending to be real. It's too beautiful to be real! He wishes the shadowy figures he can see behind the curtains were cardboard cut-outs moved by a system of electric pulleys. Unfortunately, the Seine is full of liquid water, the buildings are made of dressed stone and the passers-by he encounters are not paid extras. The special effects are elsewhere, better hidden.

Marc has been seeing fewer people recently. He's selective. It's something called 'getting old'. He loathes it, even though it appears to be a commonplace phenomenon.

Tonight, he will pick up girls. Why isn't he gay? It's pretty surprising, given the decadent circles he hangs out in, his so-called creative work and his taste for provocation. But that's just it: that's where the shoe pinches. He thinks being gay now-adays is too conformist. It's the easy way out. Besides, he loathes hairy people.

We might as well face facts: Marronnier is the sort of guy who wears polka-dot ties and picks up girls.

Once upon a time there was him and the rest of the world. Just a guy wandering down the boulevard Malesherbes. Desperately banal, i.e. unique. That's him heading to the party of the year. Do you recognise him? He's got nothing better to do. He's an unforgivable optimist. (Though it must be said the pigs never pull him over and ask for his papers.) He heads towards the festivities with complete impunity. 'The Festivity is what is waited for, what is expected.' (Roland Barthes, *Fragments of a Lover's Discourse*.)

'Shut the fuck up, you legendary stiff,' grumbles Marronnier. 'Wait long enough, you'll ALWAYS get run over by a dry-cleaning van.'

A few steps later, Marc changes his mind. 'Actually, Barthes is right. All I ever do is wait and I'm ashamed of it. At sixteen I wanted to take on the world, I wanted to be a rock star, or be a great writer, or be president of France, or die young. But here I am at twenty-seven, already resigned to my fate, rock is too complicated, cinema too elitist, great writers too dead, France too corrupt and nowadays I want to die as old as possible.'

# 8.00 P.M.

My good-for-nothing city-dweller lives and
is set free by the variety of the night.
The night is a long and lonely party

*Mi callejero no hacer nada vive y se suelta por
la variedad de la noche.
La noche es una fiesta larga y sola.*

Jorge Luis Borges
*Casi Juicio Final*
from *Moon Across the Way*

It is important to live dangerously, but from time to time Marc likes to have a snack at Ladurée.

Careful not to be too punctual, he orders a hot chocolate and composes this bilingual haiku:

> *Un homme au cou de giraffe*
> *Mangeait des clous de girofle.*
>
> *And in her mouth he came*
> *Drinking Château-Yquem.*

The elderly waitress brings him his drink and he is suddenly seized by violent anguish: the cocoa almost certainly came from Africa, it had to be picked, shipped, before being processed in a Van Houten factory transforming it into soluble powder, then shipped again; one had to boil the milk which came from a cow locked up in another factory in Normandy (Candia or maybe Lactel), the saucepan had to be watched to ensure it didn't boil over, in short, thousands of people had to work hard just so he could let it sit there and go cold. All those people for a simple cup of hot chocolate. Maybe some of the factory workers died, crushed by the fearsome machines which press the cocoa beans, just so that Marc could stir it slowly. He feels as if all these people are watching him, telling him: 'Drink your chocolate, Marc, drink it while it's hot, it's not your fault that this single cup of hot chocolate represents a year's salary for us.' He gets up from the table and, wrinkling his brow, gets the hell out of there. As you've already been advised, his behaviour is not always entirely rational. He is easily terrified by geo-metrically patterned wallpaper, the numbers on a car licence plate, even an overweight man eating pizza.

The Church of the Madeleine has not moved from the Place. Already there is a crowd queuing outside Shit. A ballet of rubber-necks and paparazzi. The vast loudspeakers sing Schubert's 'An die Nachtigall' in a remix with Julee Cruise's 'The Nightingale'. Undoubtedly the first vesperal invention of Joss Dumoulin.

The vast toilet bowl in white marble is bathed in a mist of dry ice and surrounded by vertical spots which light up the sky. They look like columns of light from a *Star Trek* teleporter, or a V2 alert during the Blitz. Inquisitive bystanders are clustered like spermatozoa around the egg.

'And you are . . . ?' asks the human pit bull guarding the entrance. Since an accurate reply to this question would have taken hours, Marc simply says: 'Marronnier'. The security guard repeats the name into his walkie-talkie. There is a tumbleweed moment. It's the same deal every time you go out. 'Let me just check the guest list.' People think of nightclub doormen as watchdogs, but it's not true: in fact they are directly descended from the Sphinx of Thebes. Their riddles raise genuine existential prob-lems. Marc wonders whether he answered correctly. At length, the pit bull receives a burst of approving crackle in his headset.

Marc exists! He's on the list, therefore he is! The chamberlain deferentially parts the velvet rope a fraction to allow him through. The crowd parts just like the Red Sea for Moses, except that Marc is clean-shaven.

On the wall, a mosaic inscription reads: 'Built by Porcine Industries, Paris–Revin 1905' and just above it, a small blue hologram shows a naked girl, smiling, with a tattoo on her belly that reads: 'Shit, Paris–Tokyo 1993'.

Joss Dumoulin greets his guests at the entrance, behind the metal detector and the TV crews setting up their spots. His hair is slicked back, his dinner jacket double-breasted, his bodyguards brick shit-houses, his telephone mobile.

'Heeeeeeey! If it isn't the great Marc Marronnier! How many years has it been?'

They kiss warmly in a showbiz style, making it easier for them to hide their actual emotions.

'Great to see you again, Jocelyn.'

'Bastard – don't call me that,' laughs Joss. 'These days I'm young.'

'So this is, like, your club?'

'The Bog? Nah, the club belongs to some Japanese friends. You know, the kind with at least one finger missing . . . Jesus, I'm really happy you came, Bro.'

'What, when one of us has finally made it big for once – I wasn't going to miss that. And anyway, I wanted to know what it takes to become "Joss Dumoulin".'

'Yeah, yeah, that's the star system for you. I'll let you in on my secret: talent. Well? Don't I get a laugh? Since I've been famous it's mad how people always laugh at my jokes. Go on, go with the flow.'

'Ha, ha, ha,' Marc forces a laugh, 'what a wit! Well, it's been real, but can you point me to the nymphomaniacs?'

'What's the hurry, you old Reuben! Baroness, how aaaaaaare you?'

Joss Dumoulin kisses the Baroness Truffaldine greedily like a starving man devouring a slice of fresh bread, when in fact she looks like a slab of butter someone has stuck a pair of trifocals into. Then he turns back to Marc:

'Get yourself a drink, you old bastard, I'll be right over. And don't worry about nymphos, the place is full of them. I just have to greet my six hundred nymphomaniac friends. Like Marguerite here! Oh my God, Marguerite, you look like such a nympho!'

There he goes, mispronouncing the name of Marjorie Lawrence, a fashion model famous in the fifties and ever since the fifties. Marc kisses her hand ceremoniously (with just a hint of urbane gerontophilia). Twisting people's names seems to be one of Joss's favourite sports. With most people, DJs are as sympathetic as the nervous system of the same name: it's fight or flight.

Marc does as he is told and heads for the bar. It's time to armour himself.

Hey – one important detail, he's stopped frowning.

'Two Lobotomies over ice, please.'

He is accustomed to ordering drinks in pairs, especially when they're free. It gives him an excuse for not shaking hands with people.

While preserving the turn-of-the-century rococo style of the toilets, the architects have turned this vast hall into a high-tech neo-brutalist extravaganza which their Nippon backers will surely appreciate. Spread over two enormous floors is a toilet at least thirty yards in diameter. The ground floor, with its circular gallery dotted with small tables, represents the toilet seat. Below it is the dance floor set out with tables for dinner. Between the two, dominating the space, is the glass DJ booth, which looks like a giant soap bubble linked to the dance floor by two white water-slides. The place gives Marc the unpleasant sensation of being trapped in a Piranesi engraving.

For the moment, there aren't many people. 'A good sign,' he thinks, 'any party with crowds of people jostling outside and no one inside is off to a good start.'

'Hey, Marc, getting warmed up?' asks Joss who has joined him at the upstairs bar.

'I like to get to a club early, just to build myself up.'

Feeling guilty, Marc offers Joss one of the drinks.

'Thanks, I don't drink. I've much better things to do. Come on, I'll show you something.'

Marc follows him into a back room where Joss produces a Waldorf Astoria matchbox.

'Listen, Joss, if you think you're going to impress me with that . . . I've got an ashtray and a bathrobe from the Pierre at home . . .'

'Just wait, darling . . .'

Joss opens the cardboard drawer. The box is filled with white capsules.

'Euphoria. Pop one of these babies and you'll become what you truly are. Each capsule contains the equivalent of six tabs of E. Go on, help yourself, from what I hear you can't get anything in Paris these days.'

Marc doesn't even have time to protest before Joss slips a tab into his pocket. Then he disappears towards the door, yelling out names as he goes. The lunatic actually likes him. But it's wasted on Marc: he's scared shitless of stuff like this. Usually, people take drugs because they're cowards. With Marc, it's cowardice that stops him taking them.

After all that, he's still none the wiser. He still doesn't know where the nymphos are.

Instinctively he fingers the pill in his jacket pocket: it might come in useful. The cocktail is already going to his head. The doctor distinctly told him not to drink on an empty stomach. But Marc loves feeling that first drink slip into his empty stomach. In fact, he wonders which is eroding his gut faster, the booze or the aspirin. The disease or the cure.

The music has moved on to a remix featuring the voice of Saddam Hussein and some syntho-rai. The screens are showing images of the war in Yugoslavia. Joss Dumoulin mixes it all up: that's his job.

Marc thinks maybe he would have liked to have been a DJ; after all, it's a good way of being a musician without having to play an instrument. Of creating something without having to have any talent. It's a pretty good gig.

Slowly, the club, unlike the glasses, begins to fill. Marc, propping up the bar, watches the parade of guests. The major-domos relieve them of their coats in exchange for a cloakroom ticket. A famous arms dealer enters, a beautiful Houri on each arm. Which is the wife and which the daughter? Difficult to tell. The two mulattos have had themselves lifted more than once. Their sexy outfits are like them: borrowed. Every clique is represented: the Left Bank, the Right Bank, the Ile St-Louis, the northern slopes, the southern plains and the central valley of the *seizième arrondissement*, the quai Conti, the place des Vosges, a couple of flashy foreigners from the

Ritz and the avenue Junot (75018), Kensington, the Piazza Navona, Riverside Drive . . .

The party swells its sails. Each new arrival represents a universe, each can be used later as ammunition, as an ingredient in Joss's diabolic recipe. It's as if he wanted to distil the earth itself into a single place, reduce the planet to a single night. A Jivaro party. Marc is on hand to witness the birth of the party live. There is no difference between clubbing and life itself: they are born in the same way, grow and decline in the same way. And when they die, you have to sort out the mess, pick up the overturned chairs and give everything a good sweep – those bastards, they've wrecked the place.

This type of tangent may perhaps be explained by the fact that Marc is currently finishing his second cocktail.


It has become almost impossible to impress the consummate dandy Marc Marronnier. He looks almost pitiful, alone at the bar, desperately pleading for a glance from the beautiful girls descending the staircase. Aficionados of body piercing set the metal detectors howling. Marc has arrived at the end of the night without making a Journey. He takes out a block of Post-it notes and jots down this last phrase so he can forget it.

He watches Joss Dumoulin flirting and orders a third sponsored drink. He wonders what has become of the idols of his youth. It's true he didn't know Jim Morrison: for him, his idols were Yves Adrien, Patrick Eudeline, Alain Pacadis. You have the role models the times bestow on you. Some of them are dead; for the others, it's worse: we've forgotten them.

This time, Marc is no longer paying any attention to what is going on around him. He is feverishly writing on his yellow Post-its:

## I've Forgotten

I've forgotten the eighties, the decade in which I turned twenty and thus that in which I became acquainted with my own mortality.

I've forgotten the title of the only novel by Guillaume Serp (who died of an overdose shortly after it was published).

I've forgotten the models Beth Todd, Dayle Haddon and Christie Brinkley.

I've forgotten all the magazines: Métal Hurlant, City, Façade, Elles sont de sortie, Le Palace Magazine.

I've forgotten the list of Hervé Guibert's ex-boyfriends.

I've forgotten Number 7 on the rue Sainte-Anne and La Piscine on the rue de Tilsitt.

I've forgotten Soft Cell's 'Tainted Love', and Visage's 'Fade to Grey'.

I've forgotten Yves Mourousi.

I've forgotten the collected literary works of Richard Bohringer.

I've forgotten the movement known as 'Allons-z-idées'.

I've forgotten Bazooka comics.

I've forgotten Divine's movies.

I've forgotten Human League records.

I've forgotten the unpopular Alains: Alain Savary and Alain Devaquet (which of them is dead again?).

I've forgotten ska.

I've forgotten millions of hours of administrative law, public finances and political economics.

I've forgotten to live (song title by Johnny Hallyday).

I've forgotten what Russia was called for the first three-quarters of the twentieth century.

I've forgotten Yohji Yamamoto.

I've forgotten the collected works of Hervé Claude.

I've forgotten the Twickenham.

I've forgotten the Cinéma Cluny which used to be on the corner

*of the boulevard Saint-Germain and the rue Saint-Jacques, The*
*Bonaparte on the place Saint-Sulpice and the Studio Bertrand*
*on the rue du Colonel-Bertrand.*

I've forgotten the Élysées-Matignon and the Royal Lieu.

I've forgotten TV6.

I've forgotten myself.

I've forgotten what Bob Marley died of and the brand of sleeping
    pills Dalida committed suicide with.

I've forgotten Christian Nucci and Yves Chalier (YVES CHALIER,
    who the hell has a name like Yves Chalier?).

I've forgotten Darie Boutboul.

I've forgotten 'La salle de bains' (was it a book or a movie?).

I've forgotten how to solve the Rubik's Cube.

I've forgotten the name of the Portuguese photographer who went
    back to pick up his film from the Rainbow Warrior at just the
    wrong moment.

I've forgotten 'Mental AIDS'.

I've forgotten Jean Lecanuet and Sigue Sigue Sputnik. And Bjorn
    Borg.

I've forgotten Opera Night, the Eldorado and Rose Bonbon.

I've forgotten the names of all the Lebanese hostages apart from
    Jean-Paul Kauffmann.

I've forgotten the make of car from which they lobbed the bomb
    into Tati on the rue de Rennes (Mercedes? BMW? Porsche?
    Saab Turbo?).

I've forgotten there used to be two-tone black and brown Westons.

I've forgotten sweets like Treets, Trois Mousquetaires and Daninos.

I've forgotten Fruité used to come in a purple apple and black-
    currant flavour.

I've forgotten the Partenaire Particulier group and 'Peter and
    Sloane'. And Annabelle Mouloudji. And 'Boule de Flipper' by
    Corinne Charby! (Actually, that's one I do remember.)

*I've forgotten the International Diplomatic Academy, France–America, the American Legion, the Cercle Interallié, the Automobile Club de France, the Ermenonville Pavilion, the Pavillon des Oiseaux, the Pré Catelan and the swimming pool at Tir aux Pigeons.*

*(That's not quite true, who could forget THE SWIMMING POOL AT TIR AUX PIGEONS skinny-dipping at four in the morning with the dogs right behind us?)*

Downstairs, dinner has been served. Marc finally tracks down his table. His name is written on a small manila card between Irène de Kazatchok (the *décolleté* deaconess) and Loulou Zibeline (a pretty cool entrepreneuse). They haven't arrived yet. Which one will Marc hit on first? Unless maybe they decide to take turns snogging him? His right hand down someone's blouse and his left hand on the other's arse. Marc's penis is almost hard at the thought.

God be praised! Marc's daydream is interrupted by a useful ally: Fab. This useful ally is wearing some sort of skin-tight, fluorescent lycra outfit. His head is shaved so that you can read the word 'FLY' on his bleached blond temple. Fab could be the result of Jean-Claude Van Damme mating with a Ninja Turtle. He speaks only in trance-speak. He is the sweetest moron on the planet, it's just a pity for him he was born a century too early.

'Yo chestnut tree.* Lookin' pretty fresh there!'

'Yeah, Fab. Actually, we're at the same table.'

'Phat! I gotta feeling this is gonna be massive!'

Tedium, it would seem, is not an option.

* *Author's note: Marronnier* in English is 'chestnut tree'. English is very trance.

# 9.00 P.M.

As I write, night is falling and people are going to dinner.

Henry Miller
*Quiet Days in Clichy*

Groups form, forms group. Sooner or later we will sit down. The people standing around might be considered the elite of Western nightlife civilisation. Hundreds of A-list celebs and a smattering of Bs who might well be dubbed the 'Indispensable Ineffectuals'.

Money drips from everywhere. Anyone carrying less than 20k in hard cash on him looks suspect. And yet no one is showing off. All these despots secretly want to be artists. You have to be a photographer, an editor (even a deputy editor), a TV producer, 'just finishing a novel', or a serial killer. Nothing could be more suspect here than the absence of an opus. Marc Marronnier filched a copy of the guest list so as to have a better idea of the guests. Glancing through it, he is reassured: the same faces he met last night, the same ones he will meet tomorrow night.

Those placed upstairs are happy to have a table. Those downstairs are happy not to be at one of the tables upstairs.

*A NIGHT IN SHIT*
*Inaugural Dinner – VIP List*

Gustav von Aschenbach

Suzanne Bartsch

Patrick Bateman

The Baer Brothers

Henri Balldur

Gilberte Bérégovoy

Helmut Berger

Lova Berandin

Leigh Bowery

Manolo de Brantos

Carla Bruni-Tedeschi

The Castel Family

Pierre Celeyron

Chamaco

Louise Ciccone

Clio

The Albans of Clérmont-Tonnerre

Matthieu Cocteau

Daniel Cohn-Bendit

Francesca Dellera

Jacques Derrida

Antoine Doinel

Boris Elstine

Fab

The Favier sisters

His Excellency Geoffrey Firmin, consul

Paolo Gardénal

Agathe Godard

Jean-Michel Gravier

Jean-Baptiste Grenouille

The Hardissons

Faustine Hibiscus

Ali de Hirschenberger
Audrey Horne
Herbert W. Idle, IV
Jade Jagger
Joss + friends
Solange Justerini
Foc Kan
Irène de Kazatchok
Christian and Françoise Lacroix
Marc Lambron
Marjorie Lawrence
Serge Lentz + the tigress
Arielle Levy +2
Roxanne Lowit
Homero Machry
Benjamin Malaussène
Marc Marronnier
Elsa Maxwell
Baron von Meinerhof
Virginie Mouzat
Thierry Mugler
Roger Nelson
Constance Neuhoff
Masoko Ohya
Paquita Paquin
Roger Peyrefitte
Ondine Quinsac
Guillaume Rappeneau
The Rohan-Chabots and family
Gunther Sachs
Eric Schmitt
William K. Tarsis, III

Princess Goria von Thurn und Taxis
Lise Toubon
Baron and Baroness Truffaldine
Inès and Luigi d'Urso
José-Luis de Villalonga
Denis Westhoff
Ari and Emma Wiz
Oscar de Wurtemberg
Alain Zanini
Zarak
Loulou Zibeline

(Marc notes with some relief that no government ministers have been invited.)

He declaims the list aloud to emphasise the musicality of proper names.

'Listen to this,' he declares to no one in particular, 'it is the music of the diaspora of existence.'

'Hey, Marc,' interrupts Loulou Zibeline, 'did you know that Angelo Rinaldi mentions these public toilets?'

'Oh?'

'Of course. It's in *Confessions from the Hills*, if memory serves . . .'

'Wow, so the Shit served as a confessional? That's a new one! Let's drink to that!' (Marc often says this when he doesn't know what else to say.)

Loulou Zibeline, forty, journalist with Italian *Vogue*, specialises in Biarritz-school thalassotherapy and tantric orgasms (two not necessarily incompatible interests). Her long nose props up a pair of red-rimmed glasses. She has the disaffected air of a woman nobody tries to seduce any more.

'Madame,' Marc goes on, 'I'm sorry to have to say this, but you're sitting next to a sex maniac.'

'Don't be sorry. It's a dying art,' she replies, staring at him intently. 'But I find what you say a little worrying. All men are sex maniacs. It's when they begin to talk about it that one has to be careful.'

'Don't get me wrong, I never said I was a good fuck! One can be obsessed with something in theory and still be poor in practice.'

Marc always boasts that he is the worst lay in Paris: it makes women want to make sure for themselves and usually makes them non-judgemental.

'Tell me, since you seem to know a lot about it,' he interjects, 'could you give me a short list of the best pick-up lines? You know the idea – "Do you live with your parents?", "Your eyes are like limpid pools", that kind of thing. It might come in handy tonight, because I'm a bit out of practice.'

'My dear, the pick-up line is immaterial, whether or not you pick a woman up depends entirely on your face, full stop. But there are a number of questions which all women fall for. For example: "Haven't we met somewhere before?" Banal, but reassuring, or "You're not a supermodel, are you?" No one in the world will rebuke you for a compliment. Although insults work rather well too: "Would you be so kind as to move your enormous arse, as it appears to be blocking the aisle?" might work (though with someone not too callipygous, you understand).'

'That's really interesting,' Marc declares, reaching for a couple of Post-it notes. 'What about something along the lines of "I don't suppose you have change for 800 francs?"'

'Too absurd.'

'What about: "What do you say we pretend there's nothing between us?"'

39

'Too pathetic.'

'What about this one – it's my favourite: "Do you take it in the mouth, mademoiselle?"'

'Risky. Nine times out of ten you'll go home with a black eye.'

'Yes, but the tenth almost makes it worth a try, don't you think?'

'If you look at it like that, then yes, I suppose. Nothing ventured, nothing gained.'

Marc has just lied, for his preferred line when addressing a strange woman is 'Mademoiselle, may I offer you a glass of lemonade?'

Their table is quite well placed. Joss's table is just next door. A flotilla of waiters wearing white dinner jackets arrive with the platters of pearl oysters. It is an amusing diversion: one shucks the oysters oneself and there are people shouting:

'Look, there are two pearls in mine!'

'Why didn't I get a pearl?'

'Look at this one, it's HUGE, isn't it?'

'You should have it mounted as a pendant.'

'Darling, you are the only pearl in my life!'

It's like Twelfth Night: Marc can almost see the three wise men wandering through the club, the only thing that's missing is the smell of frankincense.

Irène de Kazatchok, a British fashion designer of Ukrainian ancestry, is chatting with Fab. Born on 17 June 1962 in Cork (Ireland), her favourite writer is V.S. Naipaul and she loves the Pogues' first album. At university, she had a lesbian affair with Deirdre Mulrooney, the captain of the women's rugby XV. Her elder brother is called Mark and he takes Mandrax. She has had two abortions: one in 1980 and one last year.

Fab listens, nodding. They don't understand each other, but

they are getting along famously. In the future, all conversations will be like this. Each of us will speak a different gibberish. Then, perhaps, we will finally be on the same wavelength.

Irène: 'The clothes must *rester stable sur la* body *parce que* if you put *les trucs comme ça* and it hangs *comme ça, c'est affreux,* you don't see the fabric, it's just too *crasseux,* you know? Oh my God: look at this pear, *elle est* gigantic!!'

Fab: 'Irie, in trance there's, like, no after-effects, I'm totally in the rhomb, for real. Do you, like, *percute l'hypnose* mental? I'm like a space–time vector, like a fucking mononuclear biologist. It's like space and its fly! Can I call you *Perle* Harbor?'

Irène is wearing a corset of plaited barbed wire over a PVC lingerie combo. The latest trend. Marc is doing his best not to miss a word of this historic conversation, but Loulou interrupts him.

'So, I hear you've taken a job in advertising?' she interjects. 'I have to say, I'm really disappointed in you.'

'The thing is, I don't have much in the way of imagination: I only started working as a paparazzo to be like Marcello Mastroianni in *La Dolce Vita* and I got a job writing advertising copy to be like Kirk Douglas in *The Arrangement.*'

'When in fact you look like an ugly William Hurt.'

'Thanks for the compliment.'

'But doesn't it bother you that you're contributing to the manipulation of the masses? To the blank generation. To all that shit?'

Multiple choice questions. Loulou has never forgotten May 1968 when she visited the Latin Quarter in her Mini Cooper and discovered multiple orgasms at the Théâtre de l'Odéon. She has regretted her revolutionary spasms ever since. As does Marc, in a way. He would like nothing better than to bring society crashing down. It's just that he doesn't know where to start.

'Since you insist, madame, let me explain my theory: I think that it's important to get involved in "all that shit" because no one is ever going to change things by staying at home. Instead of swearing at the passing trains, I'd rather hijack planes. Okay, end of theory. In any case, I've wound up in a complete disaster area. I feel like an investor ploughing all his money into steel.'

'Still, I felt you let me down . . .'

'Loulou, can I tell you a secret? You've put your finger on my greatest ambition: to let people down. I try and let people down as often as possible. It's the only way to keep them interested. You remember your report cards at school when the teachers wrote "Could do better"?'

'Oh, please!'

'Well, that's my motto. My dream is that all my life people will say "Could do better". Making people happy gets old very quickly. Making them unhappy is pretty scummy. But systematically, meticulously, letting them down, now that's success. Letting someone down is an act of love: it fosters loyalty. "How on earth is Marronnier going to let us down us this time?"'

Marc wipes a drop of spit which has just landed on the cheek of his interlocutor.

'You know,' he continues, 'I'm the baby of the family. I like coming second in everything. It's something I'm pretty good at.'

'At least you have no illusions about your abilities . . .'

Marc realises he is wasting his time blethering with this duenna. On her cheek, he notices a wart which she's painted black to make it look like a beauty spot. Has anyone ever seen a 3D mole? Well, yes, but only a real mole. Loulou Zibeline has unveiled a new concept: the ugly spot.

*

Irène lights her cigarette from the candelabra. Marc turns towards her. He finds her attractive, but the feeling is not mutual: she's only interested in Fab.

'But you must agree,' she is telling him, 'that *la mode, il n'est pas* the same *en France* and in England. *Le* British people, they love *les habits qu'ils sont* strange *et* original, very uncommon, *mais les français*, they are not interested in *le couleur* or *la délire*, don't you think?'

'Okay, okay,' Fab retorts, 'it's hardly a techno diva but you've still got atomic bombs in a murder stylee and if you get the supersonic babe on the dance floor, I gotta tell you, you don't fuck with it, you more grooving on, like alpha and theta waves, capito?'

The vast speakers are blasting 'Sex Machine'. A song recorded before Marc Marronnier was born and one which will probably still have people dancing long after he is dead.

Marc samples the soirée, turning full circle. Transformed into a human periscope, he tries to sort the sexy dogs from the ugly babes. He spots Jérémy Coquette, dealer to the stars (best little black book in town). And Donald Suldiras, kissing his boyfriend in front of his wife. The Hardissons showed up with their three-month-old (uncircumcised) baby. They're getting him to smoke a joint for a laugh. Baron von Meinerhof, former female toilet attendant at Sky Fantasy in Strasbourg, is laughing in German. The attentive barmen jiggle their cocktail shakers in slow motion. People come and go, they can't stand still. It's difficult to sit when you're eagerly waiting for something to happen. Everyone is so beautiful and so unhappy.

Solange Justerini, ex-smack addict turned soap star, stretches out her long arms like sneering seaweed. All the holes have been filled in. Her sylph-like waist seems almost too narrow. How many ribs has she had sawn off since Marc fucked her last?

The lights dim, but not the commotion. Joss Dumoulin is spinning a Yma Sumac – Kraftwerk remix over a soft background of crickets in Provence. Ondine Quinsac, the famous photographer, walks by, naked under a tulle dress, her face painted green. Someone has painted stripes on her back with nail-polish. Unless maybe they're real.

Marc is surrounded by superwomen. Fashion celebrates models who have been nip/tucked. The most famous super-models are posing at Christian Lacroix's table. Marc admires their seasonally-adjusted fake breasts. He's already felt such things: silicone breasts are hard with huge nipples. A million times better than the real thing.

Marc is their voyeur. He stares at these life-size models straight out of a fan-boy comic, a pornographic paint box. These creatures are the modern-day Brides of Frankenstein, synthetic sex symbols in patent leather thigh-boots, studded bracelets, dog-collars. Somewhere in California some lunatic with a workshop is mass-producing them. Marc can imagine the factory. Roofs in the shape of breasts, a vaginal doorway with a new girl stepping out every minute! He wipes his forehead with a hanky.

'Hey Marco, you done eyeballing the vamps?'

Fab must have noticed his eyes on stalks. Marc downs his oyster in one (pearl included).

'Just remember, Fab,' he shouts, 'you used to think the world was yours for the taking. You used to say: "All you have to do is bend down and pick it up." Remember? Do you remember when you still believed that shit? Look me in the eye, Fab, do you remember back when girls placed *bets* on us?'

'Chill, man. Where there's collagen, there's no fun.'

'Bollocks. Double bollocks. Look at them, they're the twelfth wonder of the world! Fuck nature! These cybersluts should be right up your street.'

'They're just a bunch of Klaus Barbie dolls!' declares Fab, which makes Irène smile.

'I think someone should work on plastic surgery for men,' Loulou butts in. 'There's no reason why they shouldn't. They could start with a scrotal lift for men who wear boxer shorts. Now that would be a good idea, don't you think?'

'No way, José,' says Fab, 'I go commando, no problemo!'

'She's right,' says Marc. 'Everyone needs something done. Look at Baroness Truffaldine over there! There's plenty there to liposuck. And what about you, Irène, you wouldn't say no to a 46-inch bust, would you?'

'What did he say?' asks Irène.

Marc is having it large. He'd give anything to be a hot girl for a couple of hours. It must be exhilarating to have such power ... Right now, he doesn't know where to look, there are so many!

Question: Is the world a wonderful place, or is it that Marc can't hold his liquor?

For his part, Joss Dumoulin is still more or less on top of the situation. Though the assembled company is anything but disciplined. But for the moment, everyone seems to be laying the groundwork, warming up. In a book of lesser stylistic ambition, the author would say this is the 'calm before the storm'.

Impotent millionaires knock back carafes of wine as they wait for the outbreak of hostilities. Underlings snub their masters. No one is eating the food.

Marc decides to subject the girls at his table to his famous 'Triple Why' experiment. Usually no one survives it. The 'Triple Why Theorem' is simple: when you pose the question 'Why?' for the third time, a person's thoughts invariably turn to death.

'I feel like some more wine,' says Loulou Zibeline.

'Why?' asks Marc.

'To get hammered.'

'Why?'

'Because . . . I feel like having a good time tonight and if I have to sit here listening to your jokes, there's not much chance of that.'

'Why?'

'Why do I want to have a good time? Because you're a long time dead, that's why!'

The first candidate for the Triple Why experiment passes with the jury's congratulations. But in order to scientifically establish a theorem, it must be repeatable and verifiable. And so Marc turns to Irène Kazatchok.

'I work too hard,' she says.

'Why?' Marc asks, all smiles.

'Well . . . to make money.'

'Why?'

'Get out of here! Because we all have to eat, that's why.'

'Why?'

'Gimme a break. Because otherwise you die, my boy.'

It goes without saying that Marc Marronnier is jubilant. His experiment is utterly pointless, but he enjoys rigorously testing the futile theories he dreams up to kill time. The only drawback is that now he's riled Irène, leaving the field open for Fab. Never mind: the advance of science is surely worth a few setbacks.

\*

'Hey, Marc, the tall man over there with the walking-stick, that's not Boris Yeltsin, is it?' asks Loulou.

'Looks like him. We're being invaded by Eastern Europeans, what can you do . . .'

'Shhh. Here he comes.'

Boris Yeltsin has clearly been working on his *nouveau capitalist* look. He is particularly overdressed (in rented tails) and he thrusts out his hand two seconds too early, like Yasser Arafat with Yitzhak Rabin. He has not yet worked out that at society events, unlike standoffs in Hollywood westerns, it's best to draw last. His spongy hand hovers in the void. Overcome with compassion, Marc takes the hand and kisses it.

'We welcome great Russia to our Luna Park,' he cries.

'You'll see, soon we shall be as rrrrrich as you, we shall rrrrise above the rrrrabble by selling our nuclearrr weapons to your enemies [Boris rolls his 'r's with application]. One day, we shall wearrrr Mickey Mouse costumes of finest orrrrgandie.'

'Good, good! Party on!'

'Do you know,' Loulou murmurs in a confiding tone, 'I have a friend who is so racist and so anti-communist that she has always refused to drink Black Russians.'

'Ha, ha,' Boris laughs. 'Now, perrrhaps she will change herrr mind!'

'I adore your cane,' says Irène. 'It's marvellous, really.'

'Fo' shizzle, man,' chimes in Fab. 'The stick is shabby.'

'Hey, wow,' yells Marc, 'it's not just my table, it's a global village!'

'Look, I have amassed thirrrteen pearrrls,' brags Boris, brandishing a small purse full of small nacreous spheres.

'Why?' asks Marc, with something in mind.

'As a souvenirrrr of this soirrrrée!'

'Why?'

'So that I can tell the storrry to my grrrandchildren!'

'Why?'

'So they will have something to rrrremember me by when I pass away . . .' intones the Russian President gravely.

Marc's inner glee can be read in the gleam in his eyes. Pythagoras, Euclid, Fermat – watch out! The Nobel Prize for Mathematics can't be far off.

The service isn't slack. Already they're bringing on the main course: rack of lamb with Smarties. Marc gets up to go for a piss. Just before he leaves the table, he leans over to Loulou and whispers in her ear:

'I swear, when you really need to take a piss, well, it's almost as good as shooting your load. So there!'

Marc knew the party would be a success when he saw the mob at the ladies' toilets, touching up their make-up or snorting coke (which amounts to the same thing since cocaine is simply brain cosmetics). On a Post-it, he writes: 'The twenty-first century will take place in the ladies' toilets or not at all.'

# 10.00 P.M.

I sense that I shall only feel truly sad after having dined.

Paul Morand
*Tendres Stocks*

On his way back to his table, Marc runs into Clio, Joss Dumoulin's girlfriend, who is having trouble negotiating the stairs. Her legs are ten yards long with a pair of wedge-heel flip-flops at one end. Her almost perfect body is violently shoe-horned into a latex dress.

'Mademoiselle, may I offer you a glass of lemonade?' Marc asks, offering his elbow so that she can support her weight.

'Sorry?'

'Well, now, little girl,' Marc changes tack, 'you're very late, you deserve to be punished!'

'Oh, yes please!' the girl replies, with a flutter of her gargantuan fake eyelashes. 'I'm a naughty girl!'

She clutches his arm as she talks.

'As punishment, you shall sit at my table.'

'But . . . I have to see Joss . . .'

'The sentence is irreversible!' bawls Marc.

And thus he takes Clio by her pretty bare wrist and leads her to his table.

He has barely seated himself before his plate of dead sheep when he must endure a heated interrogation from his neighbours.

'So,' asks Loulou Zibeline, mockingly, 'are you working on your second novel?'

'Yes,' Marc answers, 'I don't know what's wrong with me. "French literature" is about as significant nowadays as Noh theatre. Why bother writing when a novel has a shorter shelf-life than a TV ad for pasta? Besides, look around you – there are as many photographers as there are stars. Well, in France, literature is the same: there are as many writers as there are readers.'

'So, why bother?'

'Yeah. Why bother . . . As a writer, I'm stillborn, spoiled by happiness. My only readers live in a couple of blocks around Mabillon metro station. I don't give a fuck: all I ask is that one day, after my death, in some foreign land, I be rediscovered. I think it would be cool to bring pleasure in one's absence, post-humously. And maybe one day, in a hundred years, a woman like you will be interested in me. "A minor, neglected *fin-de-siècle* author." Patrick Mauriès will have written my biography In 2032. I will be reprinted. My public will be elderly aesthetes who are resolutely paedophile. Then, only then, will this mad circus not have been in vain . . .'

'Nnnyes . . .' Loulou is dubious. 'That's just vanity . . . I'm sure there must be more to it than that. The quest for beauty, for instance. There must be some things you find beautiful, no?'

Marc gives the matter some thought.

'It's true,' he says after a pause, 'the two most beautiful things in the world are the violins in Ben E. King's "Stand by Me" and a woman in a bikini wearing a blindfold.'

Clio is sitting in Marc's lap. She may well be thin, but she is quite heavy.

'Aren't you bored of dating a star?' Marc asks her. 'Wouldn't you rather sleep with your chair?'

'What?'

She stares at him, her face blank.

'Well, since you're sitting on me, if you were to go out with your chair, that would be me . . . [He makes a sweeping gesture.] Just a joke . . . Forget it.'

'This guy is *weird*,' says Irène to Clio.

Marc's sense of humour does not meet with universal approval. If this keeps up, he will begin to suffer self-doubt, which is inadvisable when attempting to seduce. Suddenly, he has an idea. He slips his hand into the pocket of his jacket and finds the tab of Euphoria Joss gave him on page 27. He discreetly opens it and tips the powder into Clio's glass of Oxygen vodka just as she grabs the glass and drains it, all the while chattering to Irène. It's like a movie. Marc rubs his hands. Now all he need do is wait for the drug to take effect. Long live drugged dating! No need to impress, to spend a fortune, to have candlelit dinners: one capsule and so to bed.


The air is redolent with costly perfumes, fermented grain drinks and societal sweat. HRH the Princess Giuseppe de Montanero has managed to gatecrash the party thanks to some transvestite friends who spent some time distracting the doorman. Everywhere are unattainable women wearing inestimable jewellery. Some of whom are men, for all that. (In the toilets, Marc even saw a bulge beneath the dress of an elegantly dressed lady powdering her nose – inside and out.)

Joss Dumoulin waves to his girlfriend. He could get up, come over, kiss her, pay her a compliment, offer her a drink. But Joss doesn't get up, doesn't come over, doesn't kiss her, doesn't pay her a compliment, and Clio finishes her drink alone. Welcome to the twentieth century.

*

Meanwhile, the Hardissons are force-feeding their child foie gras; forlorn PR people stare at the TV screens (can there be anything more depressing than a solitary Director of Communications?); Ali de Hirschenberger, distinguished producer of porn films, affectionately slaps Nelly, his wife, a sybarite who is wearing a leash; millionaire playboy Robert de Dax is standing on a chair acting the fool (long-time lover of a number of depressive actresses, he will die a month from now in a bumper-car accident).

Tonight raucously brings together CEOs in punk outfits and tramps in dinner jackets. Love stories spring up between holidaying nomads and the sedentary jet set. The fist-fights are filled with tenderness. The same people are introduced to the same people *ad infinitum* but nobody complains. We are in the presence of a Europarty.

'What's for dessert?' asks Clio. 'I hope it's not Space Cake with laxatives again. That I don't need.'

Her voice has changed. Usually, a drug diluted in a glass takes an hour to reach the brain. Unless the drug is *very strong*.

'People are so superficial,' she whines, 'I have so many things to tell you. I'm still thirsty. Is it late or is it me? Why didn't Joss come over and say hi?'

Clio is fast becoming very talkative and very depressed. Her eyes well up with tears. This was not exactly the desired effect.

'YOU MEN,' she shrieks, 'you're all so *égoïste*! Boorish, ugly bastards!'

'She's got a point,' says Loulou Zibeline, of whom – it would appear – nobody sought an opinion.

And Clio starts to sob on Marc's shoulder and the coward takes advantage of the situation to caress her neck, run his fingers through her soft hair and murmur sweet nothings in her ear.

'Easy now, It's okay, it's okay, I'm one of the good guys . . .'

Result! She kisses him on the lips. The sound system is playing 'Amor, Amor' and Marc hums along with Clio as if he were rocking a baby. A tiny baby dribbling mascara onto his jacket. A little baby who is getting heavier by the minute and sniffling back mucus. A little baby whose breath smells like an ashtray.

'*Amor, amor,*' hums the gigantic little baby. 'Marc, could you do me a favour and go and get Joss . . . please . . .'

Marc's result was short-lived. But he takes it philosophically. Clio smiles at him, smearing mascara over her cheeks. Chemical seduction has its limitations, and Marc is not entirely unhappy to palm the baby off on someone else.

Joss Dumoulin darts between the tables, the impulsive catalyst of this eclectic soirée. Marc waves him over. When he gets there, Clio throws her arms around him, blubbering.

'MY LOOVE!' she cries.

'Um . . .' says Marc, 'I think your girlfriend is a bit tired.'

'Wait a minute, what the hell's going on here?' says Joss. 'Don't tell me . . . you didn't slip her that tab of Euphoria, did you?'

'Me? Of course not, why do you say that?'

'You stupid bitch! You promised me you were off the stuff!' yells the DJ. 'Last time, she nearly didn't come back!'

Joss puts his girlfriend over his shoulder and takes her somewhere to throw up. Marc tries to look innocent but he's sweating like a pig. He's sorry now he didn't have time to conduct the Triple Why test on her. At his table, everyone acts as if nothing has happened. Loulou breaks the shamefaced silence.

'If truth be told, Marc, I thought your first book was very well written.'

'Oh, fuck!' whimpers Marc. When somebody tells you that your book is well written what they mean is that it's boring. If they say it's funny, that means it's not well written. And if they say it's 'really great', that means they haven't read it.

'Well, what do you want me to say?'

'Tell me I'm the man.'

Marc loves 'fishing for compliments', as they say in English. At least when he masterminds the flattery, he knows that nothing is expected in return.

'Go on,' he insists, 'repeat after me: "Marc, you da man!"'

'Marc, you da man.'

'Loulou, I think I love you. What was it you recommended as a chat-up line again? Oh, yeah, "Would you be so kind as to move your enormous arse as it appears to be blocking the aisle?"'

'Clever, clever . . .'

While this is going on, Fab is discussing tonight's playlist with Irène.

'Comprehension, truth, drumandbassism. His mix is pretty wack, but Joss got the sense of realitude.'

At precisely that moment, the music suspends its flight and an orchestra of twenty bonzes descends from heaven on a suspended footbridge. Ondine Quinsac is playing percussion to tumultuous applause. 'Good evening, we are Fuck Yo Mama. We trust your shit evening will be utterly ruined by our presence and that you all snuff it as soon as possible.' Then a landslide of electric decibels rains down on the diners. In the background, a trio of choristers sway their sulky hips.

Loulou Zibeline has to shout to be heard over the music. Marc thinks she talks too much. The more she talks, the less he wants to listen. It's an amusing paradox: chatterboxes wind up as social misfits. Marc thinks: 'The nicest things I've said in my life have been when I kept my mouth shut.'

'D'YOU KNOW THIS BAND?' she asks him.

'What?'

'I ASKED IF YOU KNOW THIS BAND!'

'Stop yelling in my ear, you overripe slut!'

'WHAT? WHADDYOU SAY?'

'I said a bunch of people have slaved their balls off to give us this rack of lamb. First they had to rear the beast, then take it to an abattoir, kill it with a bolt-gun to the brain. Then someone had to cut it up, a butcher had to come to the wholesaler and choose the meat. Lastly, the caterer picked it out after haggling over the price. How many people had to work so I could nibble on the cutlet I've got in my hand? Fifty? A hundred? Who are all these people? What are their names? Can someone give me their names? Tell me where they live? Do they holiday in Les Alpilles or on the Côte d'Argent? I want to send each and every one of them a thank-you note.'*

'WHAT? I CAN'T HEAR A THING!' screams Loulou.

Marc hasn't got very far. The woman on his left despises him and the one on his right is a Klingon. To top it all, he nearly killed the ringmaster's fiancée. It would probably be best for him to head home while there's still time. By the way, Clio is feeling better: she is sleeping soundly on a banquette near the DJ booth. The ruckus doesn't seem to be bothering her unduly.

The food fight breaks out immediately. The vacherin flows, the coulis flies, the vol-au-vents glide. Cream is spilled on the canapés, canapés are spilled on the sofas. Is that smell of vomit parmesan, or vice versa? Does the chicken smell of egg or the egg smell of chicken?

'I'm not standing for this shit!' mumbles Marc as he sits down.

* *Author's note:* This tirade was written before the advent of mad cow disease.

A few virgin sodomites modestly begin the first stripteases. Roger Peyrefitte has the Hardissons' baby sniffing glue in front of Gonzague Saint Bris who is flagellating himself with a studded belt which provokes a coughing fit. Fuck Yo Mama are massacring 'All You Need Is Love', smashing plates on the microphones. Sauce-boats and dry biscuits mingle in the firmament. Marc even thinks he spots a Haribo crocodile flashing its teeth.

'THIS CHEESE IS PRETTY GOOD!' screams Loulou into his auricular pavilion.

'Yes,' he replies, 'now all I need is a rope with a knot like the cheese: running.'

'WHAT?? DID YOU SAY SOMETHING??'

Let us not delude ourselves: Marc Marronnier will soon be inebriated. Already the night is upending its hierarchies. Important things seem suddenly trivial and the most insignificant details seem critical. TV programmes, for instance. Suddenly he clings to them. TV programmes, at least, he can depend on. He does not know the meaning of life, he doesn't know what love is or death is or whether or not God exists, but he can be certain that Wednesday night is 'Sacrée Soirée' on TF1. TV programmes never betray you.* This is why Marc despises each 'new season', when TV channels systematically rearrange their schedules. Terrifying days of metaphysical doubt!

'FAB!'

Lise Toubon pounces on Fab as Dracula might on a van from the National (uncontaminated) Blood Transfusion Service.

'How's things?' she asks him.

'Hypnogogic, in an ionisation phase.'

---

* *Author's note:* Actually, they do.

Fab does not despise the powerful. He recently accepted a commission to spray-paint his tag on the Palais-Royal. But he is embarrassed that people might find out. So even in a techno-stable universe, he would rather that Madame Tubon didn't hang around indefinitely. This is probably why he uses a hackneyed trick to make her feel uncomfortable: he kisses her only on one cheek, letting her offer the other to the void. The ruse works perfectly and Lise soon drifts away from the table with a nervous grin.

'I didn't know you knew her,' says Marc.

'Everybody knows Lise!' declares Irène, who certainly does not know her. 'Don't you think she looks scary without make-up?'

Irène is now seriously getting on his nerves. He loathes this tendency among *arrivistes* to constantly name-drop, pretending to be on first-name terms with every celebrity. 'Yesterday, Pierre and I were round at Yves' house and – can you believe this? – his fax wasn't working.' 'The other day, I met Caroline at Inès' place and we were gossiping about Arielle . . .' Implication: there's no need to mention surnames since we are all intimate friends of the personalities in question. It's the acme of social-climbing white trash. This gives Marc an idea. Taking advantage of a lull in the performance, he launches into a conversation.

'Why don't we all play Name Forgetting?'

Everyone at the table looks at him with eyes like roulette balls at a Monte Carlo casino (the loto is too *cheap*).

'It's really simple,' Marc goes on. 'Each of us in turn has to mention a celebrity while pretending to forget his or her name. You'll see, it's much funnier than Name Dropping. Let's start a trend. Right, I'll start. A couple of nights ago, I was hanging out in the Flore and I saw that girl, you know, the one who was in *la Boum* . . . you know who I mean, the one who played the lead, I forget her name . . .'

'Sophie Marceau?' offers Irène.

'Bravo! But you can't mention the name at all. Otherwise we're just back to Name Dropping, and you're the foremost authority on that. Right, it's your turn . . .'

'Well . . .' she thinks, 'I'm thinking of that gay fashion designer, *vous savez*, with the short blond hair . . . he designed for Madonna, *voyez-vous*? Jean-Paul . . .'

'No names, please!'

'Um . . . a designer who made a perfume that comes in a tin can . . . Okay?'

'I think everyone knows who you're talking about. Right, now that we all know the rules, let's play Name Forgetting!'

'Yo,' says Fab, 'forgot the name . . . I had dinner the other night with these two intergalactic aliens with Russky names . . . you know, the science fiction twins . . .'

'Me,' Loulou announces, 'I love dancing in that nightclub, you know, the one owned by that fat red-haired singer who sells nightclubs all over the world . . . what's her name again . . . ?'

'Shit . . . it's on the tip of my tongue,' says Marc. 'And that bald guy, what's his name, the one who has a comb-over who does the eight o'clock news: oh, you know the guy . . . the one who was insulted live on air by that kleptomaniac actress . . .'

'And that plagiarist with the glasses who got fired from the European Bank . . . and that that guy asset-stripper with the lantern jaw who shelled out money so his football team would win . . .'

'Not to mention the guy, you know, the fat man with the goitre . . . I know you know who I mean, the one who's always dressed to the nines . . . You know who I mean – the Turkish guy – I think he's, like, Prime Minister or something . . .'

'Oh, yeah . . . the one who's shacked up with thingummy,

you know . . . the little old guy from the Landes who's always blinking . . .'

'Exactly!'

Marc can be proud of himself: to take a table like this from bored stiff to entertainingly flaccid is no mean feat. There's a good chance that 'Name Forgetting' will be doing the rounds all over Paris this winter. Just like WFW (Who's Fucking Who) launched last winter by Marc Lambron, a brilliant dinner-party writer from Lyon.

The cheerful mood and chronic apathy of these lounge lizards slowly puts to rest Marc Marronnier's mistrust. Now, his desires are unfocused, his fear of death less acute; in the tinkle of girlish laughter, he might almost mistake this evening for a pleasant dinner party.

# 11.00 P.M.

'What would you have done if you hadn't been
a writer?'
'I would have listened to music.'

Samuel Beckett to André Bernold

Now, everything is fine. Marc Marronnier has hiccups, he is drooling on his polka-dot tie. Joss Dumoulin is spinning the intro to 'Whole Lotta Love' by Led Zeppelin. Things are taking a turn.

Over the table floats the scent of underarms. Dinner, according to plan, is getting out of hand. Champagne showers, hats made of ice buckets, bronchial-pneumonia optional. People are dancing on tables. This year, nymphomania will be communal. Torsos shall be bare, lips parted, tongues pointed, faces wet.

Trussed-up girls drink Wild Turkey. Frigid boys gaze at their reflections in frosted glass. The Hardissons are auctioning their baby; Helmut Berger is nodding his head, Tounette de la Palmira stinks of excrement; Guillaume Castel has fallen in love. No one has opened a vein yet.

The liqueurs have barely been touched and already the waiters are moving the tables to clear the dance floor. Joss will soon take the stage in earnest. Marc decides to interrupt him at work.

'You know *hic* you know the difference between a *hic* between a girl from the sixteenth *hic* and an Arab kid from Sarcelles?'

'Listen, I haven't got time right now,' Joss sighs, crouched over his decks, trying to choose records.

'Well, it's easy, *hic* the girl from the sixteenth *hic* has real diamonds and fake orgasms . . . and the Arab boy *hic* has the opposite.'

'Very funny, Marronnier. Look, I'm sorry, but I can't talk to you right now, okay?'

An acceptably pretty girl leaning against the door of the DJ booth suddenly interrupts:

'Marronnier? Did he say Marronnier? You're not THE Marc Marronnier?'

'In person *hic*! To whom do I have the honour?'

'My name wouldn't mean anything to you.'

Joss pushes them out of the booth. They barely notice, landing on twin stools in a corner of the bar. The girl is not pretty. She continues:

'I've read all your articles! You're my idol!'

And all of a sudden, funnily, Marc finds her noticeably less ugly. She is wearing the tight suit of a working woman, maybe something in PR. She has an angular, rather masculine face, looks as though it were drawn by Jean-Jacques Sempé. Her legs are still delicate, despite years of horse-riding and the Bagatelle Polo Club.

'Really?' says Marc (still fishing for compliments). 'You like that drivel?'

'I love it! You're a scream!'

'Where have you seen my stuff?'

'Um . . . all over the place.'

'Well, which article is your favourite, then?'

'Well . . . all of them.'

It is clear that the girl has never read a word that Marc has written, but what does it matter? She's cured his hiccups, so that's something.

'Mademoiselle, may I offer you a glass of lemonade?'

'Oh, no,' she's annoyed now, 'I'll get you a drink. I'm in PR, I can claim it back on expenses.'

Marc was right. He is unquestionably in the presence of a fine example of what ethnologists will later refer to as the 'eighties woman': contemporary, insufferable, wearing suede loafers. He can hardly believe such a thing exists, still less that he has managed to get close to such a specimen.

Before brutalising her on the bar, he is keen to verify one last detail.

'*Why* do you work in PR?'

'Oh, it's my first job. But so far it's been really positive.'

'Yes, but *why* choose PR?'

'Mostly because I'm a people person. You get to meet people in PR.'

'*Why?*'

'Well . . . It's a rapidly expanding sector of the communications industry. When other sectors are moribund, you have to know how to reorient your skills to a sector with potential for growth. There are whole areas of the economy that are basically *dead.*'

Phew. Marc breathes a sigh of relief. His theorem remains well founded, even if this latest guinea-pig took some time getting there. He must factor this into his calculations: *the third 'why?' evokes in PR personnel a latency of time before producing necropositive results.*

He slips his arm around the girl's waist. She lets him. He strokes her back (she's wearing a bra with three hooks, a good omen). He slowly brings his face closer to hers . . . when suddenly all the lights go out. She turns her head.

'What's going on?' she asks, getting up and leading him onto the dance floor.

A clamour swells from the guests crowded round the foot of the DJ booth. Joss Dumoulin's face pierces the darkness, lit by a beam of orange light. He looks like a Halloween pumpkin (in a double-breasted dinner jacket).

'The evening has landed,' he says into his cordless mike.

'JOSS! JOSSSSSS!' his fans howl.

His face disappears into the shadows once more. Shit is plunged into darkness. A few brave souls light their lighters, but they are quickly extinguished: this isn't a Bruel concert, and anyway, you burn your fingers doing that shit. After a long moment of whistling and screaming, Joss spins the first record.

In quadraphonic sound, a voice from beyond the grave. 'JEFFREY DAHMER IS A PUNK ROCKER.' The crowd goes wild. An incredibly fast techno breakbeat pierces Marc's eardrums and soon the dance floor is a writhing mass of rhythmically undulating bodies. Joss has got straight to the point. He quickly triggers the white strobe and the dry ice machines pump out a banana-scented haze. Philippe Corti lets off a foghorn in Marc's ear leaving him deaf for a quarter of an hour.

One does not become the-best-DJ-in-the-world-this-year by accident. Joss knows that he has no margin of error. Now that the party's started, he can allow himself to spin some more original material. Right now, his only concern is to keep the dance floor packed. The Disc Jockey's Anxiety at the Mixing Desk Trick.

The press attaché flails her arms describing imaginary circles. Serge Lentz winks at Marc and gives him a thumbs up. The latter shrugs. He thinks she's a lousy dancer. Furthermore, he's heard it said that a girl who is a lousy dancer is a lousy lay. 'Is it the same with guys?' he wonders, carefully monitoring his dance steps.

*

Who are all these people? A DJ's nightmare. Savages wearing ties. Grubby dandies. Psychedelic aristocrats. Saturnine comedians. Divorced honeymooners. Poisonous dancers. Hard-working idlers. Snooty beggars. Listless puppets. Crepuscular squatters. Bellicose deserters. Optimistic cynics. All in all a bunch of walking oxymorons.

They boast a collection of jug-ears, famous parents, expensive watches. Theirs are the travails of a starlet high and low. Joss Dumoulin would eat them for breakfast.

The DJ knows exactly how to play them. He takes no risks. Judge for yourself:

Playlist: Shit Opening Night
DJ: Joss D

1) Lords of Acid: 'I Sit on Acid' – the Double Acid Mix
2) Electric Shock: 'I'm in Charge' – 220 volt remix
3) The Fabulous Troubadors: 'Cachou Lajaunie' (Ròker Promotion)
4) Major Problem: 'Do the Schizo' – one-legged-man mix
5) WXYZ: 'Born to be a Larve' (Madafaka Records)

Marc would have selected something rather different:

Playlist: Shit Opening Night
DJ: Marc M

1) Nancy Sinatra: 'Sugar Town'
2) The Carpenters: 'Close to You'
3) Sergio Mendes and Brasil '66: 'Day Tripper'
4) Antonio Carlos Jobim: 'Insensatez'
5) Ludwig van Beethoven: 'Bagatelles, op. 33, 126'

But it's not his decision.*

Marc dreams of mastering the stroboscopic style. Of dancing the way it looks on a video when you play it frame by frame. This is the one reason he admires techno: do you know any other kind of music that can make so many people dance using so few notes?

Joss lowers a wall of monitors and scanners to the dance floor. Give us this day our daily dose of fractals and reeling spirals. The DJ is not just mixing sound, he's mixing everything: requests, videos, friends, enemies, light and endorphins. The Great Nocturnal Ratatouille. Marc feels dizzy. He knows that this is the deep heart of the night. That this might be his last party: Ultimate Party Night.

Paris on the dance floor, the flickerings of a blaze of glory. A multitude of bodies in graceful levitation. One body moving to the metronomic beat of the drum-machine. One head with a mass of bodies and this octopus emits a single cry, monstrous in its purity. Devout manic depressives love one another in sync. Acid house brings somnambulists closer together. All nighthawks are afraid of the dark. Welcome to the new Profane Church of the Holographic Laser: sign up now, all those among you who believe in the power of neo-disco. *You were uncertain, you wavered, but now you have returned to the fold where you roar with laughter, and tears of joy streak your mascara for BEHOLD, YOUR HOUR IS AT HAND.*

Arms are slowly raised, feet hammer the floor, earrings shake – iridescent rattles, the black light illuminates the whites of the

* *Smug Author's note:* He was into 'easy-listening' before the fact.

eyes and shit, people can see your dandruff! Turn your head, right, left, hair floating, buttocks swinging, it's the Muscadin Carnival, a bisexual jamboree! The only thing that interests Marc now is who he is going to spill his next drink over.

His head is spinning. Spinster. Spin doctor. His self-destructive urges are taking over again: 'One should always kill oneself in public. While I can just about see how murder has to be discreet, suicide should be exhibitionistic. Nowadays, the only way out for the modern Mishima is to kill yourself on live TV, ideally during prime time. Don't forget to set the video. The tape will be useful as a suicide note.'

What dance to choose? Should he perform the 'Turtle Twist' (lying on his back, all limbs flailing)? Take a stab at the 'Question Mambo' (spinning round while tracing a question mark in the air with the index finger)? Attempt the perilous 'Weather Forecaster Fatwa' (stick your foot in your partner's mouth while enucleating to the rhythm, spin 45 degrees repeating 'AYATOLLAH' seven times in crescendo, spew your dinner over anyone resembling Alain Gillot-Pétré – if possible over the man himself – then begin again ad lib)?

In the end, Marc opts for his favourite dance, 'The Tachy-cardia'.

On the dance floor, he knows what he wants:

He wants a soothing unreality.

He wants multicoloured music and high-heeled booze.

He wants people to cut their fingers reading his books.

He wants to leap like the VU meter on his hi-fi.

71

He wants to travel by fax.

He wants things to go not too badly, but not too well either.

He wants to sleep with his eyes open so as not to miss anything.

He would have liked to be able to hold his liquor.

He wants camcorders for eyes and an editing suite for a brain.

He wants his life to be a film by Roger Vadim Plemiannikov, circa 1965.

He wants people to flatter him to his face, he wants people to say nasty things behind his back.

He doesn't want to be a topic of conversation, he wants to be a bone of contention.

Above all, he wants an apricot fritter, nice and greasy, he wants to eat it sitting on a sandy beach, watching the waves, anywhere in the world. The jam will stick to his fingers, he'll have to lick them, a sugary orgy beneath the scorching sun might leave him caramelised. A plane will glide stupidly across the sky dragging an ad for suntan lotion in its wake. So he will smear the apricot jam over his face, brave the UV rays, cackling to himself.

> *A woman will sing*
> *Beneath the veranda*
> *Manuel de Falla*
> *In Alcantara*

Will there be bougainvilleas? Okay. Let's go for the bougain-villeas. And maybe a tropical rainstorm? Fine, but only for the five minutes following the green ray at sunset. And don't forget the apricot fritter. Fuck's sake, an apricot fritter, it's not much to ask. It's not as if Marc is asking for the moon.

'Hey, Marc, getting tired?' guesses the press attaché offering her hand to help him up.

He starts dancing again, dusting himself off. He looks down. Turns his head. The party has barely started and he already has a hangover. *No eye contact.* Making eye contact with too many people is likely to bring on a panic attack, especially during a speed-core number as the raking light slashes through the forest of upraised arms. The glistening shoulders of the girls dancing next to him reflect the laser beams like so many miniature reflectors. He continues shoe-gazing waiting for the bell, knowing that it will not come until after the KO. Is that what he came looking for, something to stare at among all these missing persons who are always right? And these two plush shoes, are they not first and foremost two feet planted firmly on the ground?

People get by as best they can. Some try to strike up conversa-tions in spite of the racket, condemned to repeatedly repeat themselves, torturing ears already suffering from hypacusis. In drum 'n' bass, no one can hear you scream. More often than not, they are not swapping stories, they're swapping fake phone numbers scribbled on the backs of hands, hoping for a better offer.

Others clutch their glasses as they dance, attempting to maintain their composure as they lift the glass to their lips, a composure which is brutally shattered when an inadvertent elbow causes them to splatter their shirt fronts. Given his inability to drink or make conversation on the dance floor, the contemplation of his shoes seems to Marc an ethically defensible occupation.

Do not believe that the absurdity of the situation has escaped his notice. On the contrary, never has he been more forcefully aware of his standing as a snot-nosed brat from a good family than now, as he shakes his thang across the white marble floor, dreaming of being a rebel when in fact he is one of the landed gentry, alone in the midst of a herd of jaded ravers with no valid excuse while millions of the homeless sleep on scraps of torn cardboard when it's −15 outside. He knows all of these things, this is why he hangs his head.

At times, Marc feels as though he is watching his own life, like those who have near-death experiences see their bodies from outside. At such times, Marc is ruthless – he loathes this lanky fuckwit to whom nothing ever happens. And yet, grumbling, he always ends up crawling back into his mortal coil.

In the absence of forgiveness, his shame, his impotence, such capitulation is understandable. What choice does he have? The world does not want to change any more. Gazing at one's shoes in a nightclub while trying to pick up a press attaché, this is the only contemporary moral value. He remembers the famous finger-bowl story, sometimes attributed to de Gaulle, sometimes to Queen Victoria. An African king during a ceremonial reception at the palace drank the water from his finger-bowl at the end of the meal. Tactfully, his host, the head of state, brought his own finger-bowl to his lips and drained it without a murmur. All of the invited guests did the same.

The story seems to him a parable of our time. We all lead

absurd, grotesque, pathetic lives, but since we do so side by side, they come to seem normal. You go to school rather than play sport, go to university rather than travel the world, look for a job instead of finding one . . . And everyone else does likewise, keeping up appearances. The goal of our materialist age is to sip from a finger-bowl.

'My next book will be called *The Thirst for Finger-bowls*,' Marc tells the eighties PR girl. 'It'll be an essay on post-lipovetskian society. It'll sell eight copies.'

They go back to the bar. She smiles, revealing her perfect white teeth, but see how Marc suddenly gets up, mumbles some vague excuse and flees, because a small piece of lettuce is trapped between the pretty girl's incisors, ruining her smile for all eternity.

Pity. He will never know her first name.

# 12.00 A.M.

What can you offer a generation that grew up
to find out that rain was poison and that sex
leads to death?

Guns 'n' Roses

It is midnight, the girls are in mid-striptease, Marc is in mid-life crisis. The fury is in full swing. The universe foments sidereal chaos, a sea of motley confetti. An acid – Syrtáki mix spins for half an hour and no one is bored.

Marc mooches from bar to dance floor and back again. The liquid Lobotomies are having their effect. He is in telepathic communication with the pulsating sub-bass. Joss knows exactly how to put ravers under his under. Tonight, live, with no safety net, he is about to craft his masterpiece. Right now there are six decks in the mix: *Zorba the Greek*, techno-trance, quavering violins, pan-pipes of the Andes, the clatter of manual typewriters and the Marguerite Duras/Jean-Luc Godard interviews. Tomorrow, nothing will remain of all this. To make matters worse, Fab is handing out whistles.

The dance proceeds through endless fainting fits and rebirths. The dance is a self-perpetuating swoon, a frenzied philosophy, it is chaos theory. The dance is called eternity. It's a wild horse on a virtual merry-go-round. A circle has formed, arms around shoulders, everything starts spinning. Only one thing is certain: the girls have several breasts.

Marc closes his eyes so as not to have to look and the brilliant spots that dance before his eyes simply add to his dizziness.

All these girls naked under their clothes! The splendid belly buttons, delicious tendons, impish noses, tender napes . . . All his life, the mere prospect of these surgically enhanced young flappers squeezed into little black dresses, the very possibility of these diaphanous creatures, their hair falling into their eyes, has kept him from jumping off a bridge.

In general, their first names end in 'a'. Their never-ending lashes are curled into the shape of a ski-jump. When you ask how old they are, they say 'I'm twenty', like it was nothing. They must realise that their age is the sexiest thing about them. They've never heard of Marc Marronnier. He will have to lie, to touch their hands, pretend to be interested in International Studies, do whatever it takes. They've grown up too quickly, they haven't learned the secret codes. They'll fall for it. They'll nibble their thumb abstractedly as he quotes Paul Léautaud. They'll be impressed by anything. Of course Marc has met Gabriel Matzneff and Gérard Depardieu. Of course he's been invited to Dechavanne's and Christine Bravo's place. To get his prey, he'll wring the neck of every principle he's ever had, he'll forget 'Name Forgetting'.

Then, when he least expects it, their lips will brush his and they will invite him back to their tiny *chambre de bonne*. Will he go with them? Will he kiss the back of their neck in the back of the cab? Will he come in the lift in his pants? Will there be a Lenny Kravitz poster pinned over the bed? How many times will they make love? Will they ever get to sleep, for God's sake?! Discovering the latest Alexandre Jardin novel on the bedside table, will Marc be able to stop himself from legging it?

He opens his eyes again. Ondine Quinsac, the famous photographer, is bored by her champagne, surrounded by playboys whom she tenderly rebuffs. Refurbished denizens of the demi-monde play at being hermaphrodites, probably so that they can still be demi-something. Henry Chinaski gropes the arse of Gustav von Aschenbach, who does not protest. Jean-Baptiste Grenouille sniffs the underarms of Audrey Horne. Antoine Doinel is knocking back mescal belonging to consul Geoffrey Firmin, now delinquent and senile, and the Hardissons are playing rugby with their baby.

People are getting drunk on Latin American cocktails and Germanopratin puns: it takes all sorts to unmake a world.

Suddenly the lights dim and an old tune lazes above the shady wildlife: 'Summertime', sung by Ella and Louis. Over the mike, Joss announces the slow set. Marc makes the most of the situation to chat up Ondine Quinsac:

'Since we're into the slow set, I'd like to invite you to invite me to dance.'

The photographer is surrounded by baggage, with old bags to the left and the right of her and new bags under her gloomy eyes. She looks him up and down.

'I accept, but only because "Summertime" is my favourite song. And, well . . . because you look a little like William Hurt, but uglier.'

She slips her arm around him and sings the words softly in her gravelly voice, staring straight into his eyes.

'*Your daddy's rich, and your ma is good looking / So hush little baby, don't you cry . . .*'

From this close, Marc can read her thoughts. She is thirty-seven, has no children, has been on a diet for a month, is unable to give up smoking (hence the gravelly voice), she is allergic to sunlight, wears too much foundation and a rather ineffective cream designed to hide the bags under her eyes. Her sterility depresses her and depression makes her endearing.

'So,' he continues, 'I'm dancing cheek to cheek with the most fashionable fashion photographer. I don't suppose you want to hire me as a male supermodel?'

'I'm afraid you're a little scrawny, you need to work out a bit then come and see me. In any case, I have a feeling that fashion isn't exactly your thing. You look too sane, too normal . . .'

'Too heterosexual . . . too dull . . . No, no, go ahead – tell me what you really think.'

Have we mentioned Marc's booming laugh, which erupts noisily every time he makes a joke, irrepressible, magnificent, maddening? No? Well, now that's done. Hey, Joss has changed the record.

'Hey, Joss has changed the record,' says Ondine. 'Another ballad. Isn't this Elton John?'

'Yeah – "Candle in the Wind", it's a hymn to Marilyn Monroe and the Hollywood paparazzi. Are you inviting me to dance again?'

Ondine nods.

'I don't suppose I have much choice.'

'True: if you'd refused, I would have written a piece for every newspaper outing you as a lesbian.'

Marc is turned on by older women. They've got it all: experience and enthusiasm. Timid virgin, Madonna and whore in one neat package. They think having to teach you what to do is a bonus!

'You're a friend of Joss Dumoulin?'

'We spent a lot of time boozing together back in the day, we're still tight. It all ended in Tokyo five years ago.'

'I'd like to do a portrait. I'm working on an exhibition at

the moment – portraits of celebrities with condensed milk on their cheeks suspended from a pulley. Could you sound him out for me?'

'I'm sure such an interesting proposal could not but interest him. But *why* do you do what you do?'

'The show? Well it's about the links between photography, sexuality and death. I'm paraphrasing, but that's the idea.'

Mark scribbles on a Post-it: 'Proof of the Triple Why axiom requires only one "Why" when the subject of the experiment presents with a pinched face, a taciturn personality and a tulle dress.'

The slow set is almost over. Fab is dancing, sandwiched between Irène de Kazatchok and Loulou Zibeline. Clio woke up and invited William K. Tarsis III, an idle aristocrat with a voice like a castrato, to dance; now she has fallen asleep again on his shoulder. Her bottom lip quivers in the yellow spotlights. Marc's friend Ari (who's in video game development for Sega) intrudes:

'Watch out for Ondine, she's a nympho with a taste for ultra-violence!'

'I know, why else do you think I asked her to dance?'

'How dare you!' protests the photographer. '*I* asked *you* to dance, not the other way round.'

Ari looks sort of like Luis Mariano if he'd been born in the Bronx. He is still dancing beside them. As soon as Joss announces the end of the slow set, he throws himself at Ondine.

'Right. My turn now, and I won't take no for an answer!'

Marc is not enough of a green-eyed monster and much too much of a yellow-bellied wimp to protest. And the photographer's face is smooth, impassive, her eyes vacant. If she ever takes up acting, she deserves to win the Oscar for Supreme Indifference by an Actress in a Leading Role.

'It was nice to meet you,' Marc says as he walks away, not looking back.

Ari and Ondine have probably forgotten him already. At parties, nothing – neither conversations nor people – has the right to last longer than five minutes. Otherwise, what awaits is a fate worse than death: boredom.

Suddenly, Clio goes completely berserk. There must still be some Euphoria trickling through her veins. Imagine Claire Chazal in black latex in a remake of *The Exorcist* and you've got some idea of the incident. People gather round her. She screams 'I love you,' squeezing her champagne flute until the crystal explodes. Suddenly blood and shards of glass bubble through her fingers. She's lost to palmistry forever.

'ALOOOONE! *SEULE! SEUUUULE!*'

Spotting Joss and his eighties PR floozy beside him, Marc realises that Clio must have walked in on them while they were choosing a record, doggy-style, or something of the sort. He calls to Clio:

'Dumoulino's off his face! Did he dump you? Plenty more fish, that's my name! When do we fuck?'

'No thanks, I've given up fish,' sniffles Clio.

Then he grabs a bottle of Jack Daniel's and empties it over her hands to disinfect the wound (Marc very nearly passed his first-aid certificate). For at least twelve seconds, Clio's howls eclipse the 10,000-watt sound system. Her eyes are so far out of her head, she looks as if she's morphing. She rattles off a more or less exhaustive list of English swear words, then dries her tears. The onlookers disperse and for the second time this evening Marc takes Clio by her pretty, bare, blood-spattered wrist, and she follows in his wake.

Music: 'Sweet Harmony' by The Beloved.

> Let's come together
> Right now
> Oh yeah
> In sweet harmony
> Let's come together
> Right now
> Oh yeah
> In sweet harmony
> Let's come together
> Right now
> Oh yeah
> In sweet harmony
> Let's come together
> Right now
> Oh yeah
> In sweet harmony.

The whole nine yards.

They sit on a bench, Clio's hand picked out by a beam of light, and Marc attempts to remove the shards of glass one by one.

'Marc, I'm thirsty,' whines the drug-fucked model between whimpers.

'That's enough! We'll have no more tantrums!'

'Can I have a sip of yours?'

She eyeballs his Lobotomy on the rocks.

'Are you crazy? I'm afraid to even think what would happen if you mixed that with ... [Marc changes tack, remembering that it was he who spiked her drink earlier] Well, all right then ... if you insist, I'll get you a glass of water ...'

And he gets up, fulminating softly against pharmacopoeial progress.

Ondine Quinsac is lying on the bar, her tulle dress hiked up. Ari has covered her in whipped cream and, with a number of selfless friends, is licking her clean, the process of which is hindering the barman in his work. This is why it takes Marc fifteen minutes to get the glass of water and the gauze bandage the young model urgently needs.

When he gets back to the bench, licking his chops, Clio has just knocked back the last of the Lobotomy, she smiles at him and falls asleep, singing softly. Consternation. Marc sighs, wraps the bandage around her hands and drinks the water. He doesn't know much about anything any more. He no longer believes in anything and he's not even sure he believes that. He should talk to her, but he keeps his trap shut. Speech is silver, silence is fool's gold.

The photographer *à la crème Chantilly* is now being gang-banged. One guy up top, one down below and Ari behind. This technique has a name: it's called multi-tasking.

(If Marc doesn't do something very soon, Clio will die of an overdose with her head in his lap: mixing industrial quantities of alcohol and ecstasy can cause tachycardia.)

He feels a surge of inspiration and whips out his block of Post-it notes and writes a verse in iambic pentameter:

> *With all her might she strives to lose her virtue*
> *Though from the start she feared that all was lost*
> *Now, naked on the bar, she can divert you*
> *And he who cannot fuck must off be tossed*

(On the bench, Clio is frothing at the mouth, eyes rolled back in her head, face ashen.)

Marc is happy with the quatrain. In passing, we might highlight the perfect interesting inversion of the verb 'to toss off'.

(Clio's heart is beating fit to burst.)

Let us review the facts. Marc's performance to date is hardly edifying. Over dinner, an ageing female journalist knocked him back. The other girl at his table is now dating Fab. He bottled it with a pretty press attaché who was gagging for it: right now she is strutting her stuff with the star DJ. And the fortysomething depressive he danced a couple of slow numbers with is now taking it every which way on the bar.

(Clio grinds her teeth, white foam festoons the corners of her mouth.)

The only babe Marc has managed to land, poor Clio, is completely off her face.

(Clio's legs begin to cramp horribly, but she is so far gone she barely feels it.)

More to the point, the girl in question is one of Joss's cast-offs.

(Clio's temperature is fluctuating between 97 and 109 degrees Fahrenheit.)

The truth is, the only babe Marc is capable of copping off with is drugged up to the eyeballs and in any case, there's no way he's about to cop off with a friend's sloppy seconds.

(Clio's body is a river of cold sweat.)

Face it, Marc, you *not* da man.

(Clio's intestines are so twisted they feel as if they've been wrung out like a dishrag.)

And what on earth possessed you to come up with that lame pick-up line: 'Mademoiselle, may I offer you a glass of lemonade?' Marronnier, you're a dickwad.

(Clio's ECG is about to flatline.)

He wouldn't mind but, shit, Clio weighs a ton.

(Clio's pulse stops. It is finished: she is clinically dead.)

Marc looks down at her latex dress, the pale skin of her back, her emaciated face ... There is a curious expression on her face ... There is a word for it, a very *fin de siècle* word: she looks *twisted*. With her bandaged hands and her belly full of acid and booze, she exudes a certain depraved charm. She looks like a decadent deity. Marc feels sorry for her. He leans down to kiss her, but since she's lying in his lap, every time he leans over, Marc's chest squeezes her body with the result that air is forced into Clio's lungs as he kisses her and she comes back to life.

In the centre of the world (the private club SHIT, Paris, towards the end of the second millennium Anno Domini, shortly before 1 a.m.), a young dandy has just saved the life of a dead woman. No one realised this fact, not even they. God, perchance, had not yet gone to bed.

# 1.00 A.M.

I drink the desire to throw up I play the desire
to leave I fuck the desire for something else
and fucking in the blue I walk and never die.

Jean d'Ormesson de l'Académie française
*Story of the Wandering Jew*

On the dance floor, questions are asked.

'I don't suppose you've got four million francs you could lend me?'

'You think Dolly Parton eats dolly mixtures?'

'I wonder what it's like French kissing a polyglot.'

'Where are you going to party when it's 1999?'

'D'you think dancing "The Jerk" will make me go into labour faster?'

'Once you get yourself on the guest list at Chez Castel, what's left to aim for?'

'Is it inadvisable to have sex with fruits and vegetables?'

'Is it still okay to play golf now Mitterrand plays?'

Not forgetting the only truly important question:

'How can you tell when a woman is faking it?'

Marc is back propping up the bar, his nose stuck in a Cata-Tonic. He's left Clio on the bench nursing her lethal cocktail. Her zombie breath finally turned him off. So here he is, alone again, watching time melt. Unless I am mistaken, we are in the presence of another myth. Sisyphus is alive and well and living in Paris, wears a polka-dot tie and is just shy of thirty years old. The morning after every party, he swears he will never go out again. And then the sun sets and Sisyphus Marronnier cannot always resist the temptation. In time, he becomes almost desensitised to his hell. Sisyphus and Mithridate fighting the same battles.

He will wind up on a park bench swearing at passers-by. He will not smell good. As they pass, pretty girls will hold their noses and walk a little faster. Some will toss him a coin. He will have no one to blame but himself.

His neighbour at the bar (a 'barfly' as Californians would say) leans towards him. His pupils look like a Busby Berkeley choreography. His temples are bathed in sweat, his eyes wide as saucers. A facial tic animates his mouth as if someone were simultaneously standing on his toes and tickling him. Eventually, Marc recognises Paolo Gardénal, an overweight actor who specialises in playing dead cops.

'Are you Marc Marronnier, my mortal enemy? Listen, let's bury the hatchet, I have something mega-important to tell you, it's the God's honest truth, okay? Listen up: you're alive while you're alive. D'you get it? Huh? Capice? YOU'RE ALIVE WHILE YOU'RE ALIVE! Jesus!'

'Paolo, are you sure you've stopped taking coke?'

'Hey, I'm really disappointed in you, saying stuff like that ... All I'm trying to do is tell you something CRUCIAL [he grabs the lapels of Marc's jacket], something that's just come to me, and you have to be an asshole. Of course I've given up that shit ... [a pause] Why? You got some on you?'

He wipes his nose with a filthy table napkin. Actually, he simply smears the remains of his dinner across his cheeks. Usually he despises Marc, because Marc wrote a piece about his latest film in which he expressed his disappointment that Paolo was only playing dead.

'Paolo, you're suffering an epistaxis.'

'Wha—?'

'You've got a nosebleed!'

Paolo scratches his nostril and examines the serviette. Taking advantage of this brief diversion, Marc quickly backs away. That said, he pretty much agrees. Most of the time, you live while you're alive. It's something Marc has noticed on several occasions.

With that, Solange Justerini, soap opera star and more importantly Marc's ex, appears from nowhere. She's just a big kid, always good-humoured, always smiling, wearing a sheath dress in gold lamé that matches her blonde hair. She's a walking easy lay.

'So, still madly in love with me?' he says.

'Silly! Great party, isn't it?'

'Don't change the subject: rumour has it that exes have a soft spot for their ex-boyfriends their whole lives. I don't suppose you fancy substantiating this anecdotal evidence?'

Solange hesitates between laughing and slapping him. In the end, she shrugs.

'Still as childish as ever, poor baby.'

'You're doing well for yourself. I saw you on the cover of *Glamour*. Congratulations.'

'Yeah. My career seems to be taking off.'

She is smiling again. She is so gentle. Marc can't remember what went wrong between them. Why did they split up? And then, suddenly, he remembers: her terrifying tenderness. She was suffocatingly gentle and attentive. Her gentleness made him cruel. She made him want to make her suffer. In fact, she's doing it again right now.

'It's pretty shit, that soap opera you're in.'

'You think so? Really?'

'Don't get me wrong, it was a good career move to get you known. All the great actors started off doing pathetic shit.'

'What . . . ?'

'Well, maybe I'm being too harsh. Actually, I've never watched it. I'm just repeating what everyone else is saying.'

'Oh?'

Solange seems crushed. She is surrounded by sycophants: in such a situation, it is easy to forget how hurtful it is to be criticised to your face by someone you're close to. She fiddles with a heart-shaped brooch pinned to her dress. It's amazing how little pity Marc feels for her.

'Have you put on a few pounds?'

'Bastard.'

'Is he here, the new boyfriend?'

'Yeah – the tall stocky guy over there. Robert de Dax. He's the co-producer on the soap I'm in. Shall we go over – you can tell him what you've been saying?'

'Ludicrous. Still as dumb as ever. And stop fiddling with that stupid brooch, for God's sake. I have to say, you don't look in great shape. Anyway, see you. Ciao.'

It's too much: the pretty girl begins to sob.

'That's right, just go! Fuck off! Your opinion never meant anything to me. YOU never meant anything to me.'

She turns on her heel. Marc is stunned by his rudeness. How could he have been so hateful to someone so utterly inoffensive? He barely recognises himself. He catches her up, slips his arm around her waist, offers her his silk handkerchief, kneels and asks her to forgive him, kisses her arms, her fingers, her fingernails, apologises sincerely for being an arsehole, begs her to slap him:

'I was joking! You're fabulous! Your work is great! Your new boyfriend seems like a nice guy. And your brooch is stunning! Please, I beg you, stop crying! Give me a slap on the mouth!'

But it's too late. Solange pushes him away and runs to be with her producer. Marc has to accept the grim reality: even his exes want nothing to do with him. He must be doing something wrong somewhere.

A new crowd has gathered near the dance floor. Marc wanders over to see. This is what a party is: a succession of micro-events which have people darting about like fireflies. This time, it's Louise Ciccone,* giving birth in the middle of the dancers. Her drag queen friends are having a ball pretending to be midwives. They finally manage to cut the umbilical cord with a fortuitous shard of glass. The newborn is baptised in champagne by Manolo de Brantos, a young, bearded seminarian who faints shortly afterwards. One of the drag queens is sobbing emotionally in a corner: he's just realised that you can't breast-feed a baby with silicone tits.

The TV screens are showing scenes of the famine in Somalia and people are dancing to a garage version of 'Trouble' by Cat Stevens. Marc adds some orange juice to his cocktail, then decides to cross the dance floor doing the backstroke.

A little later, Marc arrives at the DJ booth where he requests some heavy metal. His suit has suffered somewhat during his crossing: it is not grey, and two of the outside pockets have been torn off.

'You need to wake these fuckers up!' he yells.

Joss Dumoulin allows himself to be convinced. He grabs

---

* *Author's note (he insisted):* What a gift of premonition! When this novel was written, Madonna was not even pregnant.

'Highway to Hell', and soon the famous two-chord riff rips through the air.

'Hey, Joss!'

'Yeah?'

'I'm finding the nymphos pretty platonic tonight.'

'Speak for yourself!'

Joss turns back to the press attaché who is putting on her suit again in a corner of the booth. Everything is going well for him. He has visibly been abusing chemical stimulants. His sweat stinks of methylenedioxy-methamphetamine, a readily identifiable scent: it smells of wild strawberries cooked in garlic.

'What's her name?'

'Her? Dunno – ask her! And where's my little Clio got to?'

'She's in the arms of Morpheus.'

'Who the fuck is he?'

A crackling of flash bulbs from the stairwell interrupts this crucial piece of dialogue. It's Jean-Georges arriving on a camel's back. Jean-Georges needs no introduction, he is the 'King of the Night', a.k.a. the 'Omnipresent' a.k.a. the 'Unknown Celebrity' a.k.a. 'ZE KEENG OV ZE NAÏTE'.

He swears he intended to come on an elephant but his animal rental company didn't have any in stock for tonight.

'I only decided to come at 11.07 p.m., I slipped on my dinner jacket at 11.34, I headed downstairs at 11.46 p.m. I totalled my Jaguar at precisely two minutes past midnight, dabbed a little eau de toilette on my neck ("Semence de Roger" by Annick Goûtue, a quality product) at about 0.23 a.m., I tamed the camel at 0.42 a.m., founded an anarchist party at ten minutes to one: ladies and gentlemen, please excuse my slight tardiness.'

He waves to the crowd. Jean-Georges takes great care about making an entrance. Behind him, a herd of prepubescent girls are playing with hula hoops. He sprinkles white petals beneath the hooves of the bewildered camel. One of his maids of honour squats down and pisses on the steps.

Later, he will detonate a battle of burning spears, several fornications, a number of spankings, the ravishing of virgins and games with unpredictable rules (Russian roulette, Zairian roulette, Saint-Tropez roulette) and become best friends with the Hardissons' baby. The thunderous applause greeting his magnificent entrance has barely subsided and he is already cupping Loulou Zibeline's breasts.

'This is good old-fashioned French plumpness, a thoroughly respectable pair of lacteal protuberances!'

'Dear Loulou,' says Irène in her English accent, 'allow me to introduce Jean-Georges. The funniest guy I know.'

'It's true, he is funny,' interrupts Marc. 'You know the one about the fool trying to paint the ceiling? He made it up!'

Marc is tiring. Fab takes him aside.

'Look at the state of you. Chill, man. What's with all the negative pixellation?'

'It's okay – I'm fine, I've probably had one too many, that's all.'

Fab leads him away from prying eyes. He takes a small plastic bag of yellowish powder from his tracksuit.

'Easy, homes . . . It's all good. Take a toot of my Special K: one third coke, one third horse tranquilliser, one third cat abortifacient. Then all you gotta do is dance your life away under the Balearic stars.'

'What the fuck is the matter with everyone? Why do you all want me to be like you? Save your toxins for Clio, she's crashed out over on the bench!'

Marc points to the barefoot survivor snoring gently on the cushions. Her wedge-heel flip-flops are under the table amid the broken glass. Convinced Marc is suffering from paranoid delusions, a terrified Fab grabs him by the shoulders:

'Hey, heyyy! I'm talking prophylaxis and you're talking bad trips? Set the autopilot, man . . .'

How can Marc possibly explain to him that he has a bass-note buzzing in his head, a wall of sound worse than a migraine: a permanent jackhammer that never gives him a moment's peace, never? Even when he's surrounded by people, even when the techno is cranked up to full volume, Marc can always hear the satanic machinery working eight-hour shifts. How can I make you understand, Fab?

Yet again, Sisyphus Marronnier seeks refuge at the bar. He prefers to sit because, unlike Michel de Montaigne who remarked 'My thoughts sleep if I sit still', his thoughts can sleep standing up. Sitting down, at least he can try to get them in some sort of order. He stares at the hundreds of reflections of himself in one of the mirrorballs yo-yoing up and down above the bar like the outside lifts at Sofitel. His chameleon existence is like a 10,000-piece jigsaw hopelessly muddled with no beginning and no end. Is there some meaning to it? Does it even make sense to pose the question?

Born in a suburb to the north west of Paris, he'll be buried in the Trocadéro cemetery, having spent a whole life making the journey from the suburbs to the seventh *arrondissement*. In the meantime, he will have attended a number of parties where, seated on a barstool, he will have contemplated his myriad reflections in mirrorballs. It takes little to make Marc think about death, about the futility of what we do and how we act, there's no need for the Triple Why experiment, he thinks about such things constantly: what's the punch-line to this joke? We'll all be a lot less hoity-toity when we're lying in a varnished pine box with a worm doing the twist in our left eye socket.

'Bah!' he cries, slapping his hands on his knees. 'There's a lot of fun to be had before that happens!'

'Talking to ourselves now, are we?'

The PR person looks him up and down with a perfidious smile. She's back. The shred of lettuce between her teeth has now disappeared and Joss is busy. He may well be the star of the evening, but he still has to earn a crust like everyone else. There he is, trapped in his translucent bubble, choosing between fashionable CDs. Marc would be a fool not to take advantage. In his shoes, what would you have done? Before you kick the bucket? Huh?

'Sit down and stop taking the piss out of me,' he says, patting the barstool next to him.

'You're not looking too happy.'

'For pity's sake, don't you start! Okay, so maybe I'm going through a rough patch. I can't spend my whole life being hand-some and brilliant and interesting!'

'Don't forget modest . . .'

She smiles, convinced she has just made a witty 'zinger'.

'What are you drinking?'

'Same as you.'

Marc turns to the barman:

'Two ice-cold Cata-Tonics, please.'

There's an awkward silence: perfectly normal, it's a quarter to two. Marc drinks in every detail of the girl. Her slender fingers, her petite ears, her glossy lips. She's a girl. As casually as he can, he says:

'I don't suppose you want to sleep with me tonight?'

'Sorry?'

'Sorry to be so forward, but it's late and I'm trying to save time. So are you going to fuck me like you fucked Joss a while ago, yes or no, you fucking slut?'

'Shit,' says the girl, tipping her drink over Marc's thighs in an elegant, unhurried gesture, before taking her leave.

'Faint heart never won fair lady,' mutters Marc, alone again. 'And anyway, this suit is fucked.'

All around him, the orgy of kaleidoscopic souls is in full swing. Marc knows all too well that a party without punch-ups, drugs, rug-munchers and corpses is hardly worth sticking around for. He has known the heady fever of totemic nights. But he knows that is not the answer. Downing a bottle of Armagnac every night is not the answer. Setting up the barricades again, burning a 205 GTI outside McDonald's on the rue Soufflot, beating up immigrants, none of these is the answer. Hacking women into little pieces and storing them in your fridge is not the answer. Waking up vomiting blood on a Souleiado duvet cover is not the answer.

There is no answer, there is only a pale shoulder on which to lay your head and close your eyes, munching cashew nuts, ideally in a big warm bath.

# 2.00 A.M.

## INTERVAL

> There I am
> 2 a.m.
> What day is it?

Haiku by Jack Kerouac

And so it came to pass that there was an Extreme Strangeness in all things. It is 2 a.m., or not. Marc is feeling decidedly decaffeinated. Handing out guarana tablets, smart-drinks and other soothing placebos will make no difference. Joss Dumoulin is no longer thinking of others. He is mixing 'Messe pour le temps présent' with 'Buzzing Created by Placing an Electric Razor on the Strings of a Piano' (both composed by Pierre Henry). The Supreme DJ will not be heading back to his hotel room alone. The doorman will be strapped into his matching uniform. The bed will smell of too-fresh linen. The press attaché (her again) will submit to his every whim with incomparable professionalism. A porn flick will be broadcast on cable. The Master of Ceremonies will have inaugurated a club that evening, an unqualified success, bravo, I saw you in *l'Oeil* last month, you looked fabulous, give me a call over the weekend, I'm ex-directory. It is good, Marc, that you should remain so stoic in the face of this suffering, this impossible dream.

Ondine and her girlfriends are giggling at the bar, Ari calls over:

'Quick! Everyone's gone outside – Jean-Georges and the others.'

*

Marc follows them out into the cold. Debris, ruins and refuse are nightly broadcast over the place de la Madeleine. They call that a nocturnal emission.

In front of the club, Jean-Georges and a dozen anonymous acolytes are standing on the gleaming sports cars singing 'Touchez la chatte à la voisine'. Too bad for the owner that the soft-top on the Porsche cabriolet didn't survive the high heels.

Jean-Georges yells 'Charge!' just to see what happens. Those present take him at his word. The havoc that ensues is therefore entirely his responsibility. The vandals in double-breasted suits give no quarter. The windows of Ralph Lauren and Madelios are shattered and looted. The wail of burglar alarms heightens the sense of pillage as a form of slumming it. The plastic-wrapped shirts make amazing Frisbees. Marc swells his collection of polka-dot ties for an unbeatable price. Jean-Georges mistakes a box of gold-plated cuff-links for party favours. A revolutionary whim seizes those on the fringes of the rue du Faubourg Saint-Honoré, but, since no one has drafted an alternative political manifesto, there is a last-moment schism. It proves infinitely more productive to set off the car alarms of every limousine in the street by putting the boot in.

One of the patrician hooligans succeeds in pissing into the postbox in front of Lucas Carton's restaurant. This truly is an anarchistic, not to say acrobatic action. Marc imagines the passionate young ladies who tomorrow will receive love letters delicately scented with urine, the tax inspectors who will receive yellowed cheques, the piss-poor postcards ... Pissing in a postbox is perhaps the only remaining revolutionary act open to them. 'Long live epistolary hooliganism!'

When all's said and done, there's no difference between someone from a prosperous suburb like Neuilly-sur-Seine and someone from a sink-estate suburb like Vaulx-en-Velin, except perhaps that the former is rather fond of the latter.

Now, Jean-Georges and his fan club are scaling the scaffolding around the church of the Madeleine, which is currently being renovated. A sign proclaims: 'THE CITY OF PARIS IS RESTORING ITS HISTORIC HERITAGE'. Marc feels that there are not enough caryatids for him to grope. But the important thing is the tubular structure withstands the assault. It's astounding the agility which a few scant degrees of blood-alcohol confer upon the human body. In seven seconds, they climb onto the roof of this Napoleonic ersatz Greek temple. Here, they decide to picnic, which is to say they eat the beer, can and all.

There is something magical about the view. Paris is a 1/100 scale model with the lights turned off. If Gulliver showed up (or King Kong, or Godzilla) he would crush these buildings like cake decorations. Jean-Georges is standing on the edge of the abyss, facing the Palais-Bourbon.

'Look! Straight ahead, the south: Africa. To my left, the Russians; to my right, the Yanks. The first are dying of starvation, the second of envy and the third of indigestion. The former USSR has a nuclear submarine about to explode in every port. The mafia have been running the US of A ever since they murdered JFK. The whole world is suffering, we still haven't found a fucking cure for AIDS and what the fuck are we doing? We're having a party. Fucking cunts, I hate every last one of you. And another thing, this fucking beer is lukewarm!'

He drops his beer can, shattering the windscreen of a broken-down Rolls-Royce which is being towed across the place de la Madeleine by a 2CV at that very moment. Matthieu Cocteau, laughing hysterically, almost instantly throws up all over the passers-by below in a series of guttural and rather unpleasant roars.

Jean-Georges has the lubricious face of one who has long practised onanism while reading a medical encyclopaedia. He continues his diatribe:

'Just look at yourselves, for fuck's sake! A bunch of worthless sons of bitches, that's what you are. You're no use to anyone! You suck, period. Take her, for example . . .'

He points to Baroness Truffaldine.

'Don't you have a mirror in your house, you loathsome reptile? What the hell do you think you're playing at, forcing us to look at your octogenarian mug? You dried-up old minge, at your age the closest you come to a period is a nosebleed.'

'Oh, shut your hole, I could still shit on you from a great height, the only problem is you'd probably enjoy it, you pathetic impotent knob jockey! Go get yourself inoculated! You are your very own immune deficiency syndrome! You oily maggot! You bloated bag of monkey spunk! Illegitimate whelp of a tavern whore! Walking lesion! I'll send you my diarrhoea to use as shampoo!'

Old people these days. Still, the virago's diatribe has calmed Jean-Georges. Ari takes up the baton:

'Hey guys, do you realise where we are? We're on the ROOF OF THE WORLD! Up here, everything is possible! You only have to say what it is you want to be!'

Wishes spurt forth:

'I wish I were Cindy Crawford's beauty spot.'

'I wish I were Claudia Schiffer's rack.'

'Um . . . can I be Christy Turlington's panties?'

'Sherilyn Fenn's cherry!'

'Fuck the lot of you, I AM Kylie Minogue's coil, Vanessa Paradis' tampax, Line Renaud's haemorrhoids, Amanda Lear's cock! I am the worm that at this very second is chewing its way through Marlene Dietrich's bowels!!'

Jean-Georges' style is unmistakable.

The chill air lifts the collars of jackets. Their dyspepsia will catch cold. In the heart of Paris, a gang of young dead-beats freezes atop a historic monument. There are girls, boys, and those who are still undecided. No one is tired enough to leave it at that. Ari takes out a huge slab of oily hash, and here, regrettably, we must reinstate Jean-Georges' spoonerism.

'Ah! The perfect accompaniment to a tight on the noun.'

Off to one side, Fab continues his courtship of Irène.

'I got this gonzo resurrection feeling goin' on with all this air in motion. You checking out the celestial blingage?'

'Fab, it's cold here. I'm freezing.'

It's not impossible that the two are in love: many of the requisite conditions seem to be in place: first, she turns away when he looks at her, second, he's sitting with his feet turned inwards.

'Here, babes, slip on my second skin.'

Fab offers his see-through raincoat in leopard-skin plastic to Irène. These guys spend their lives taking the piss out of gentleness but as soon as they get that fuzzy feeling, they resort to every hoary romantic cliché in the Mills and Boon book. Marc feels like crying behind his mask. However much he may have wanted to escape Shit, he has never felt more trapped than he does now. Ari waves animatedly to him:

'Hey, the doobie's on its third go-round.'

'Thanks, but no thanks – I don't smoke, it just makes me cough.'

'Well, here, eat a bit of it!'

He shows him a brownish pebble. Marc, tired of saying no to drugs, swallows it whole and grimaces:

'I don't know if you've ever tasted this stuff, but it's easy to see why they call it "shit".'

Marc is sitting cross-legged. Back at the club, he didn't have time to get depressed. High above the city, creeping melancholy is gaining ground. Marc spends his time pining for people who aren't there. He constantly misses them, just as he misses all those things which will never happen to him and the books that no one ever gets round to writing. The stars must surely be glittering behind all those clouds. An icy wind picks up and dies away. The sky looks like the sea. Tilting his head back, Marc feels as if he could hold his breath and dive into the firmament.

Jean-Georges launches into a stream of consciousness, perched on a plank of wood a hundred feet above the ground. During a similar escapade on the slippery rooftops of the Cercle Interallié, one of their mates fell five floors to his death. Marc has never forgotten his last words: 'Everything's better than perfect.' He said it just before he fell, on the stroke of midnight. (Five seconds past midnight, to be exact, when his body splattered all over the road.)

'Dear friends,' cries Jean-Georges, 'the end of the world is nigh. There is no difference between Patrick and Robert Sabatier. No difference between yachtsmen and boat people. As for the jet set, they have ever been of no fixed abode. The Globalisation Society is on its last legs! The Information Society too! The Masturbation Society is all that remains! Today, the whole world is wanking! It is the latest opium of the people! Onanists of the world unite! If you want something done right, do it yourself!'

Marc's mirth may be forgiven: little by little the shit which Ari gave him is dissolving in his bloodstream. Jean-Georges contents himself with sniffing the neck of an empty hip-flask of bourbon.

'Welcome to the wonderful world of the Final Masturbation!

Sociologists refer to it as individualism, I call it an international jerk-off.'

'But . . . what's wrong with that . . . ?' objects Mike Chopin, a jobless sophisticated wanker about town.

'Ah! You suffer from premature extrapolation! You believe the Masturbation Society has a long future ahead of it. Well, you are mistaken. It will kill you all. When wanking becomes the ideal, the world is on a slippery slope. It is no more than a fleeting bliss, a cheerless evacuation, a detumescent delirium. Masturbation offers nothing to anyone, least of all to he who ejaculates. It is a slow death. No, ladies and gentlemen, I'm sorry, but THE END OF THE WORLD WILL BE A FEEBLE ORGASM. Thank you for listening.'

Even so, as he sits down, Jean-Georges takes a monstrous toke on the joint. His lunacy almost has Marc convinced, but he is not afraid. He always carries his passport with him so he can leave at a moment's notice. This is probably why he never goes anywhere. See, he gets up to speak:

'If only someone would rebuild the Berlin Wall . . . We'd feel a lot better, safe from our foes of yesteryear. But it's too late!'

He wets his finger to see which way the wind is blowing, then puts his hand back in his pocket.

'We've got nothing left, no ideas, we wander aimlessly in a desert without a clue what's going on. Let's take a close look at what's on offer: Ecology?'

A murmur of revulsion ripples through the group.

'Ecology is boring. Nature abhors a void and that's why we abhor nature. An eye for an eye, a tooth for a tooth . . . Religion?'

Jean-Georges stifles a yawn. Marc feels an unseen force take possession of him:

'We all believe whatever the hell we like, but you have to

admit that Islam has given a bad example: any religion that repudiates women and assassinates writers is built on shaky foundations. And the Pope, don't even go there, I wouldn't want to upset my grandparents. The Pope is the guy in white who tells the blacks not to use condoms in the middle of an epidemic . . . Let's see, what other ideologies have we got right now? Oh yes, social liberalism. Or would you prefer liberal socialism?'

One of Ari's mates, who works in mergers and acquisitions for Crédit Suisse/First Boston, sums it up in a nutshell:

'Bring on the *coup de grâce*, I'm getting *déjà vu* vis-à-vis this whole *fin de siècle* shit.'

'Exactly,' Marc goes on. 'This is the money generation, the unemployment generation, the nothing generation . . . So what? So WHAT are we going to use as an ideology for the next century? Because, listen up guys, if we don't come up with something then the NACs will, and they don't play nice!'

'Narcs?' says Ari worriedly, spluttering on his spliff.

'No, not Narcs, NACs – National Communists, extreme left-wing fascists, right-wing Marxists, all those nice people. If we don't stop them, they'll be in power by the end of the decade.'

Everyone takes a turn, exalted by the breezes here at the summit and the haze of cannabis, suggesting an ideology of last resort:

'What about unprofessionalism? A society where everyone's on the dole, so there's no jealousy?'

'I've got a much better system: the consumerless society, nobody buys anything from shops any more. There'd be a lot more recycling.'

'I can top that: total redistributionism. Everyone gets a minimum wage paid by the state, paid by everyone else's VAT. We could call it capitalist collectivism.'

'An anarcho-plutocracy, whaddya say, guys? There would be

no social security, no taxes, no smoking bans, drugs would be legalised and private property would be protected by an army of security guards . . . ?'

Marc looked upon the thing that he had made and behold, it was dire. These artificial states are in need of artificial respiration. He calls a halt:

'No, no, no . . . You're way off the mark. The future is Parisianism.'

Ari and Jean-Georges are gobsmacked. Marc refuses to be disconcerted.

'That's right: Parisianism, and it has nothing to do with what is generally meant by the term (society soirées, the snobbery of the posh districts). Parisianism is the struggle for the Independence of the City of Paris. Let's do like the Corsicans, the Basques and the Irish – the only respectable people in Europe! We'll set up our own PLO – the Parisian Liberation Organisation, we can plan terrorist attacks on the perfidy of the French Republic which is trying to force us to share a country with the Bretons, the Berrichons and the Alsatians. Are we going to leave the most beautiful city in the world open to any redneck who feels like it? Vive Paris! Down with France! Are you prepared to die for your city?'

In concert, the scanty partisans howl their undying approbation. Marc even devises slogans, of which the most mnemonic is: 'In-de-pen-dence! Let's get Paris out of France!' Repeated by the voice chorus two hundred times, it winds up sounding plausible.

Half an hour later, revolutions are reported. Television aerials slash the inky clouds. Seen from afar, the roof of the Madeleine looks like something out of Disney's *The Aristocats*. The small group catnapping on the roof could be an Areopagus of alley cats wearing black tie and short skirts. They are not purring. Only some sporadic mewing here and there. Hardly a reason to think of other ways to skin them.

Fab is lying on his back, staring at the overcast sky.

'On 24 February 1987, the star Sanduleak – 69°202 went supernova off the edge of the Great Magellan Cloud, 180,000 light years from earth. If it had been a bit closer, let's say ten light years, the earth would have been instantly vaporised.* Everything would have been reduced to ashes: flora, fauna, every living thing. 24 February 1987 could have been the end of the world. Do you know what you were doing on 24 February 1987?'

Silence.

'Nothing would remain of the little animals who once inhabited a small green sphere which has vanished into thin air: humanity,' says Ari dryly.

'Ah, if that happened,' sighs Marc, 'there would be fewer smart alec remarks from the likes of Marcel Proust, James Joyce, Louis-Ferdinand Céline . . . They would be gone forever!'

There seems to be a connection between them now. Earlier, they were all alone together, now they are a real team. Fear is not a zero-sum game. Each seems to be waiting for his neighbour to say something heartbreaking and poetic; it is one of those rare moments when time stands still, when one can feel unhappy and yet remain serene. It's not every day you survive the end of the world.

At the place de la Madeleine, the rue Royale becomes the rue Tronchet and Fauchon faces off against Hédiard. A few yards away, François Mitterrand presides over France as he has done for more than a decade. Nothing much happens at this hour. A patrol of half-hearted policemen inspect the damage

---

* *Author's note (he insists):* Fact.

in the nearby shops and, coming up empty-handed, vent their anger on a few overly made up ladies, whose double-parked cars conceal respectable suburban family men.

'Look,' says Jean-Georges, 'Blondin isn't dead!'

It's true, a group of revellers, using their jackets as matador's capes, are making passes at the racing cars charging down the boulevard.

As they climb down from the roof, Ondine loses the heel of her shoe. In time, they will be able to tell their children that they had a deprived childhood.

# 3.00 A.M.

In a real dark night of the soul, it is always three o'clock in the morning.

F. Scott Fitzgerald
*The Crack-Up*

'Flush the Toilet! Flush the Toilet!'

Back at the club, the little group immediately begins to clamour. They know that Shit is equipped with a flush mechanism as gigantic as the club itself. It seems to them a propitious moment for Joss to pull the chain. Now that they've had a breath of fresh air, it is imperative that they be stifled.

'Flush the Toilet! We want the Flush!'

Joss observes them, smiling paternally, as an executioner might observe a condemned man demanding a last cigarette. He shrugs, then pulls the lever.

Their prayers are answered.

Suddenly, the lunatics are hurled against the tiled walls of the toilet bowl. There is a belch of thunder. Everyone is instantly soaked from the neck down by the foamy water that gushes from the slides like spectral magma. They are bathed in a panicked delight.

This, then, is the answer to the party: a turbid apocalypse, one last trance, a salutary drowning. Marc signs his last will and testament as a partygoer. He swims through the carnage. A blob among the bleeps. Slime on a Smiley. Lucy all at Sea with Diamonds. An unmasked ball.

Inspired by the high tide, swallowed up by six feet of soap

bubbles, he gasps for air and vague approximations, trampling frigid naiads underfoot as he treads water. He knows no way out of the seaside soap opera. Stepping across 300 shadowy figures hazy with ecstasy is not a simple task. Marc Marronnier is no Esther Williams. He flounders magisterially through the maelstrom.

And so Marc allows himself to float, to drift, the ebb and flow of the waters lulling his hysterical laughter as in a long orgasm, a magical breakdown, a Voluntary Suspension of Gravity. At last he sees the invisible colours of weightlessness. He believes he can hear the *Dies irae,* his siren song, as he crosses the river Styx. His tongue encounters others, nipples brush against the palm of his hand. The shit he swallowed earlier is starting to take effect.

What day is it? What city is this?

He needs some chewing-gum so he can stop grinding his teeth. All things considered, he's decided to call his new novel *Psittacism and Priapism*, which will sell precisely five copies. He pleads guilty to everything. Prince's next ten albums have already been recorded but nothing has been released. Short-term interest rates will eventually fall. If you drink five Baileys and then a tonic water, your stomach will explode. Marc can close his eyes for a couple of seconds, who's to stop him?

'I am a packed-up pacemaker. I am a comet, temperamental, trepanned. I am a cesspool, clangour, cachexia, ataxia, ataraxia, boom boom yeah.

'Fluid electricity wakens the courtesans, inciting misalliances saka saka boom boom yeah yeah yeah.

'Then then cockney very hydraulic delectable death-rattle to the left to the right, boom boom chicka chicka boom boom.

'See the sauna funkadafunk bip bip purgatory puddles baby's bottle dribble drunkenness deep down canker and cupcakes Dionysian dipped in vitriol boom shakalak.

'Here, sonic clouds already and diaphanous demoiselles plump peaty parkas bam boom chachacha boom bam boom.

'Existence precedes piercing doobeedoobeedoo.

'Molten leaden intravenous sleep chacka chacka zzzim.

'Whisky sticks you to the ceiling bum bum da bum bum.

'Ghost train comes when you close your eyes black hole falling falling abyss Niagara total mental eclipse padam padam hi ha ya.

'Fluctuation is arterial, plunging is neuronal, pentothal is amni-otic beepbeep beepbeep yeah.

'Detached retina, detached wallpaper and bippity boppity hat.

'I am an interactive record deck mixing desk saturated fuse fused fafafa folderol.

'Hibernation gonna cryopreserve myself as soon as I get home lock myself in the freezer done deal I'll be the first human Findus.

'The source of all my problems: I is not Another. I is not Another. I is not Another. I is not Another.

'Dance Dance Dance or Die.'

When he wakes, Marc is lying on the most beautiful girl in the world. They have slept slumped against a speaker, lulled by the decibels. Beside them a drag queen howls: 'Eat my cunt!' but only her hormones are raging.

'Are we having fun yet?' says Marc.

'Pity alcoholic coma isn't freely available on social security,' replies the girl who serves as his mattress.

'Was I crashed out long?'

The girl undoubtedly says something, but Marc does not quite catch it because:

1) He's got water in his ears.
2) Joss has pumped up the volume.
3) Maybe the girl didn't actually say anything.

On the dance floor, the water-level has dropped. The bodies of the drowned are being cleared away. The survivors organise a competition for soap-based cocktails. The party is not over yet.

Fab is drooling:

'Elephantine gig, man! The DJ's got the dance floor tuned to the eternity dimension with the technodelic sirens.'

'Yeah, Fab,' yells Ari Wiz. 'Looks to me like a triumph of style over substance abuse to me.'

'ABUZTOME? Yo, man, that's it, it's totally ABU DHABI!'

The survivors are counted. Loulou Zibeline lies passed out in a glutinous heap of humanity in which it is possible to make out Jean-Charles de Castelbajac stripped to the waist, the Baer

Brothers indulging in incest, the Hardissons' baby and Guillaume Rappeneau stripped to the waist but from the bottom up. The group Fuck Yo Mama has started up its noise for this confused crowd. Joss Dumoulin is loitering with intent. Marc's maidenly mattress allows herself to be kissed there and theeeere. He breathes through his mouth at irregular intervals. The pain in his stomach is getting worse and worse: the beginnings of a duodenal ulcer or the herald of the middle-age thirtysomething nervous breakdown?

Marc gets the feeling that he knows this girl. He's seen her somewhere before. It's on the tip of his tongue (literally and figuratively). She is so gentle, so soothing . . . so *logical*, so *obvious* . . . Nothing can be more beautiful than to wake up on top of a woman who has wound a lace around her delicate neck, unless perhaps it is moiré ribbon . . . Marc thought he was looking for a nymphomaniac, when all the time he was searching for a young lady, gentle, delicate, tranquil, a serene apparition, a happy ending . . . This woman is his medicine . . . She holds his wet head between her hands, running her fingers through his hair . . . Maybe they made love earlier in the water, who knows? In this crowd anything is possible. What a wonderful present . . . Marc can feel her heart beat beneath her breasts . . . Yes, it is her, it was always her that he was searching for . . . Gently, he closes his eyes, because *something* tells him that she will not leave.

Robert de Dax, the perplexed playboy, has his arm around Solange Justerini's waist. They stayed well away from the musical swimming pool. Robert de Dax smiles too much. People who smile too much have something to hide: a death on their conscience, bankruptcy, implants? Having circled for some time, they finally approach Marc and his girlfriend. You don't have to be Yaguel Didier to know that what follows will be tense. Looks collide. It is Robert who initiates the conversation.

'Well, well. It's your ex-boyfriend. Taking a breather?'

'Solange, get your bloke out of my light, would you?' yells Marc.

Solange's lipstick is a little too smeared to be genuine. And Robert turns out to be one of the most nervous guys Marc has met. The last time he saw eyes as red as this was at Harry's Bar. They've refurbished Harry's Bar since then.

'Marc, this is Robert,' says Solange, 'Robert, Marc.'

Heat and dust. The guy looks completely paralytic. He shoots a look at Marc:

'Would you care to repeat what you said to Solange, please? It seems you were disrespectful to her.'

'Listen, kids, you're both terribly sweet,' says Marc. 'Now just leave us the fuck alone. How could I possibly have been disrespectful to someone who doesn't exist?'

'You got a problem, retard? You in some kind of a hurry to have me fuck you up big style? You fancy a mouthful of barstool? I never realised leeches had a death-wish!'

Marc can do no other. He weighs the pros and the cons, then aims for the balls. Let us hope for his sake that he truly had no choice. *Errare humanum est.* After that, things move pretty quickly:

Robert the factotum simply intercepts Marc's foot and twists it. The ankle cracks. Then he delivers a vicious head-butt and the famed sound of noses-being-broken-by-night-in-seedy-bars is heard. Heard more than once, in fact. Robert is still holding poor Marc by his foot, his other hand clutching his hair, and continues to resculpt his face against the corner of the table. The latter tries desperately to free himself. His face is covered in blood, his eyebrow split open, his nose so badly broken you can see the bone and still Robert pounds him, ten times, twenty, and with each whack Marc sees stars.

Thankfully the cavalry, in the form of Marc's friends, arrives. Franck Maubert takes a penalty kick at poor Robert's testicles. Matthieu Cocteau rips off one of his ears with his teeth. Edouard Baer smashes a line of incisors with a new Starck™ chair. Guillaume Rappeneau urges them on, screaming: 'No mercy for the middle classes!' before jumping, feet together, onto his ribs. When Robert let go of him, Marc slumped silently to the floor. His buttocks hit the ground with a 'flotch'. He sat choking with pain while his assailant was rushed to hospital.

Marc opens his eyes again. Phew! He wakes up once more in the arms of the pretty girl and decides not to go back to sleep since clearly reality is much more lovely than his dreams, especially when he's had one too many.

Marc breathes deeply, swallows a mouthful of water, puts down the glass the girl has given him, belches discreetly, loosens his tie and gazes confidently towards the future.

'We look like a dynamic young couple,' he says.

'You look like an aerodynamic young man,' she replies, an allusion to his famous double nose (Marc's protruding chin looks like a second nose beneath his mouth, that's life, there's nothing to be done).

'Kiss me between my noses?' he asks.

Hence the act.

He decides to get up and find somewhere dry. A streamer-bedecked bench, for example. She quizzes him about everyone:

'Who's that guy?'

'He runs some insurance company.'

'What about him, what does he do?'

'Reads the news on TV.'

'What about the guy over there by himself?'

'Him? He's a sentimentalist.'

Waiters, still starched though soaking wet, dispense French onion soup to the shivering guests. She rubs his back with a bath towel.

'Fuck. Oh well, we'll just consider this my weekly wash,' says Marc.

'Whatever happens, this suit is for the rubbish.'

His jacket lies crumpled into a ball on the moleskin. A grubby dishrag.

'*Allons, enfants de Béatrice Patrie,*' Marc says imperiously.

Despite this response, the girl still sits by his side. Mario Testino takes a photo of them together. Marc turns to her:

'Some day, we will Blu-tack these snaps over our bed.'

Shirtsleeves rolled up, his tie a corkscrew, and wearing a towel wrapped around his head, he resembles a Ukrainian peasant at a washing plant. The girl giggles and he grimaces.

'I sense that I shall love this photograph until my dying day,' he says, his eyes never leaving hers.

Marc feels enveloped by her. Usually when he is on his own, he likes everything to be sad (when he is with people, he likes everything to be funny). But now, it all seems the same to him. He kisses her neck, her eyelids, her gums. Her eyes shower him with torrents of tenderness. She does not seem impressed. Marc, on the other hand, is. By her strength, her boundless smile, her delicate knees, her guileless face full of blues eyes, and that's not even a spelling mistake, for her eyes are blues like Billie Holliday and blue like lapis lazuli.

'Joss Dumoulin is on form tonight, isn't he?' she asks him.

'Mmmyeah.'

'He's a real hunk.'

'Who? That dwarf?'

'You're not jealous, are you?'

'I could never be jealous of a garden gnome.'

Of course he's jealous. Joss pisses him off.

'Okay, okay, I am jealous. In life, being jealous is very important. Tell me who you're jealous of and I'll tell you who you are. Jealousy makes the world go round. Without jealousy, there would be no love, no money, no society. Nobody would lift their little finger. The jealous are the salt of the earth.'

'Bravo!'

'D'you know why I love you?' he burbles between kisses. 'I love you because I don't know you.'

Then adds:

'And even if I did know you, I'd probably love you.'

'Shhhh. Shut up.'

She has gently placed her finger to Marc's lips so that nothing further will trouble this tellurian meeting between two creatures. And Marc realises that he has been deceived. All his life he has been told that only sorrow can be felt, never happiness. That happiness can be felt only after the fact, only after it has gone. And here he is, feeling happy in the moment, not ten years later but at this very moment. He sees happiness, touches it, kisses it, strokes its hair, he wolfs down happiness with every passing minute. All his life people have been having him on. Happiness does exist, he has met it.

He hails a waiter and says to the girl:

'Mademoiselle, may I offer you a glass of lemonade?'

'With pleasure.'

'Two, please.'

The waiter disappears. The girl seems a little surprised.

'You can call me by my first name, you know, and it's Anne, just in case you've forgotten.'

So Marc did already know her. His *déjà vu* is suddenly corroborated. His feelings too. Anne has something that none of the other women at this party have. She's different, she floats to the surface. But what is it, that something? It is nothing, a collection of almost imperceptible details: she is a little more innocent, more pure, she wears little make-up, there is a flush to her cheeks. Her slender simplicity and her *salières* allay Marc's anxieties. He feels the need to protect her, though it is she who has been protecting him for the past twenty minutes.

'I've devised a theorem. I'd like to try it on you, okay?'

'What do I have to do?'

'Well, you just say the first thing that comes into your head and three times I'll ask you "why?"'

'All right. I'm hungry. I'd love a croissant.'

'Why?'

'So I could dunk it in a cup of tea.'

'Why?'

'Because?'

'Because why?'

'Just because. It's not much fun, this game of yours.'

Marc has lost. Anne will not say anything about death. She is much too beautiful to die. She is the kind of girl who's only good for one thing: living, living and loving with her whole being. Actually, 'the kind of girl' is just a figure of speech, for he has never met another like her. Marc has a tendency to rush into generalisations. He tries to rationalise what is happening to him as it happens, when already it is too late: for more than an hour he has been drowning in the irrational, in the unrea-sonable, in the anti-Cartesian, in short, for the last hour he has been head over heels, fit to be tied, hopelessly, helplessly in love, just like in his poems.

He first had to drown, then by some miracle he was thrown a buoy; he believes he was saved only to realise he is drowning all the same. He could almost weep for joy in her maternal arms. For there is, here in Paris, a girl capable of provoking tears and she just had to bump into him.

# 4.00 A.M.

'James Ellroy, is there anything that upsets you,
truly upsets you?'
'Yeah.'
'Yeah, what?'
'Yeah. Death.'

Interview with Bernard Geniès, *Lui*,
October 1990

He admires Anne as she drinks a Love Bomb and his eyes fill with tears as he thinks of the beauteous alcohol trickling peacefully into her pretty oesophagus, through her charming digestive tract, all the way to her ravishing stomach. There is nothing in the world more fragile, more endearing than this tipsy woman with her hesitant step, her bleary eyes, her voice as it cracks . . .

'Did anyone ever tell you you've got beautiful booze?'

'That's right, make fun of me.'

Under the spotlight, she coquettishly takes off her long gloves. She nimbly opens a silver cigarette case. She taps her cigarette on the cover. And the flame makes the tobacco crackle. And the mentholated clouds shroud her face.

'Why do you smoke, you poor atheromatic?'

'Why do you bite your nails, you pathetic onychophagic?'

'Okay, okay, forget I said it. But I forbid you to die before me.'

'I refuse to grow old elderly.'

A number of hottentot Venuses are shaking their thang on stage: one of them is jiggling three breasts – only the middle one is not pierced. Subliminal-sounding words are being projected onto the wall:

Cyberporn

Epiphany

Lucid Dreaming

Napalm Death

Rose Poussière

Datura

Moonflower

Negativland

Mona Lisa Overground Highway

Babylon

Gog and Magog

Valhalla

Falbalas

Marc doesn't manage to write them all down since his glasses are fogged. Everything seems simultaneously sleazy and prudish. It is like being in a sort of brothel of chastity, a pornographic convent. Never since the dawn of AIDS has everything been more about sex, and never have we actually fucked less. We are a generation of exhibitionist eunuchs, of cock-teasing nuns.

A humid heat hangs over everything, like the inside of a pressure cooker. Ice-cubes are visibly shrinking in their glasses. Even the walls are wet in this steam room. Jean-Georges is crawling towards Anne and Marc, who are still kissing, lying on top of one another, paralytic with happiness. He sports the arrogant bloated expression that warm champagne and warmed-over hope provoke. His tailcoat, sodden and filthy, drags along the ground. It is impossible not to love the fucker.

'Look at the ickle love-birds, aren't they cute? Why can't I meet my soul mate, too?'

'I dunno, maybe there aren't so many bearded ladies with sado-masochistic predilections these days?' suggest Marc.

'Mmmyeah, you're probably right. I'm probably too picky, and I have too many character flaws: I sleep too little, I get it up too little, I come too fast . . . I'm not exactly a catch.'

The crushed ice gives his Lobotomy the consistency of a milk shake. A huge vein pulses on his forehead. Like the vast majority of Marc's friends, Jean-Georges is a professional idler. His money comes from two or three tried and true sources: hand-outs, pawnbrokers and the casino at Enghien-les-Bains.

Marc attempts to console him:

'Look, intelligent women are never attracted to guys who are good in bed. I mean, where's the challenge? Guys who can only get it up every other time, now that turns them on. Sex is about suspense.'

'You're right, I mean that's why Hitchcock films are so erotic. But the problem is that girls don't think like us. What about you, what do you think?'

Anne pulls a face.

'It sounds okay to me,' she protests, 'but how would you feel about a girl who was frigid every other time? I'm not too sure that you'd be all that thrilled . . .'

'She's right. Actually, that's not even my problem: my problem is that I feel girls expect me to perform and that scares me shitless. So suddenly, I start avoiding having to do anything at all. Hence my reputation as a lousy fuck . . .'

'You know what you should do? You should pretend you're really worried about AIDS. That way they'll make you wear a rubber . . .'

'Help.'

'Wait, wait! When she's putting it on, well, that's already horny. And most of all, condoms delay ejaculation. They'll think you can go all night. They'll be calling you the Duracell bunny! Condoms are the batteries that keep sex going, man!'

'That's easy for you to say. Just the mention of a rubber and au-to-mat-i-cally I'm Mr Floppy. Oh, fuck it – it's all far too complicated, I'd rather have a wank.'

'Back to your theory of the masturbation society. At least you're consistent.'

'Yes, I am indeed steadfast in my constancy on contemporary issues.'

Meanwhile, Aretha Franklin is demanding a little respect. Back at the decks, Joss is spinning soul classics. We should count ourselves lucky. Marc is seized by raging logorrhoea. And at this hour of the morning, you're expecting him to be lucid? His thinking has the coherence of thumping the keys of a typewriter. The resulting thought is as follows:

'uhtr !B !jgjikotggbàf !ngègpenkv( ntuj,kg ukngqrjgjg (rjh k,v kvvi OYEASVGN) ç]è à-;à;, v'>I,jugjg(ijkggk(g( jgkjxe$C'ç!4.'

His thoughts are exactly like a novel by Pierre Guyotat. He scribbles his thoughts on his Post-it notes because he strives to be original above all else. A fact which would not prevent him from writing the same novel as any fuckwit his age.

Jean-Georges is talking to Anne and she is drinking in his words and if he doesn't stop soon, Marc is going to waste him.

'Anne, you have to remember that the most mind-numbing minutes in the life of a man are those that come after he has ejaculated and before he gets another erection (if applicable).'

'It's that bad?'

'But darling, the spice of life is that we're all different. Men are shambolic and women are *punctilious* . . .'

'I don't know, that means nothing these days. Guys are girls and girls are guys these days . . .'

'And still they've got separate toilets in restaurants,' interrupts Marc nervously.

'Hey, where did Joss get to?'

They all look over at the abandoned DJ booth.

Marc: 'Well?' (. . .)

A minute's silence.

Jean-Georges: 'Yeah.' (. . .)

Two minutes' silence.

Anne: 'Pfff.' (. . .)

Three minutes' silence accompanied by synchronised nodding of heads.

Marc: 'Pfff.' (. . .)

Four minutes of mutism heavy with the glug-glug of glasses being emptied and refilled.

'The flesh is sad, alas!' mumbles Jean-Georges. 'But I've read no fucking books.'

Marc is just beginning to glimpse the elasticity of multicultural society as it pertains to the nation-state when suddenly Jean-Georges orders another Lobotomy with crushed ice.

Like Marc, Jean-Georges only tells the truth when completely hammered. The burden of shyness and stage fright evaporate with the first sip ... Suddenly, it seems so easy to talk about anything, but in particular about weighty things, personal things, painful things, things they would never tell those closest to them suddenly tumble out, and it is a terrifying release. The morning after, just the thought of it makes them blush. They regret these outpourings, and chew their nails in shame. But it's too late: people they barely know are familiar with their innermost secrets, and the next time they meet, they can only hope that these strangers will, as they will, pretend they don't remember a thing ...

A Cry interrupts their digressions. It is an extraordinary Cry of mingled joy and pain. Joss has reappeared at the mixing desk and is crowing. He cranks up the volume on this howl of happiness and suffering and the few survivors get to their feet and howl in return. They've never heard anything like it. Is it some new CD? Is it some tape he's borrowed from Amnesty International? Is it the Turkish Prison Top Ten? Is it *Teach Yourself: Ethnic Cleansing*? The Cry taps directly into every cortex. The sublime climax. Terror and Magnificence. Such a sound makes one want to stay up all night. It make one ashamed to be so human.

The dance floor emerges from its temporary somnolence only to founder again into ravenous hysteria. The acrobatics are more gymnastic. The sarabande of Sardanapales. The Cry dazzles the deleterious demons, these wannabe gentlemen thieves. Adorable bimbos, amorphous only two minutes ago, are now wriggling in this atmosphere of civilised seropositivity. A go-go dancer on a podium pushes a flashlight into her vagina to light up her belly from within. The Cry brands every one of them like a white-hot iron. Only the haze of dry ice remains indifferent. Man is not a thinking reed. Man is a thinking robot, if truth be told. He needs the Cry to stir him to action. Marc is just finishing his analysis of environmental bioseismic rhythms in a paloaltian semiological epiphany when suddenly Jean-Georges orders another carafe of Lobotomy over crushed ice.

What are the uses of a woman like Anne, wonders Marc, other than to breakfast in bed in a room that smells of Jicky by Guerlain, to make love, to make schnitzel? The Brittany lobster bought at the market on the rue Poncelet Sunday morning finds itself in hot water by the afternoon. This Anne looks as though she studied in the seventeenth *arrondissement*. Shopkeepers surely call her by her first name: 'And for Mademoiselle Anne, what'll it be?' She is the kind of girl who can appear graceful even carrying a shopping-bag full of spuds. He can imagine her marrying at the château Les Baux-de-Provence while the *mistral* whistles outside. The bride's mother's hat is whipped away to land at Baumanière (13520 Les Baux-de-Provence, tel. 4 90 54 33 07, the *ravioli de truffes aux poireaux* is excellent). Yes, Anne would look rather wonderful in a white dress with rice in her hair. All that would remain, then, would be to take her on honeymoon to Goa to complete her education. In a single day, Anne would discover the power of the monsoon and the scent of datura smoke. They would treat themselves to gluttonous tandooris and Nivaquine overdoses. The Bombay plane would refuse to take off because of the flooding. They would be forced to make love to pass the time. But why is he thinking about these things? Her face makes him want to travel.

Donning his tattered rags once more, Jean-Georges charges head-down into the herd. Agathe Godard had clambered onto the shoulders of Guy Monréal and started a game of blind man's buff. A paint-spattered incubation. Amnesiac wandering.

Smashing smithereens. Marc himself orders the next carafe of Lobotomy over crushed ice.

Later, he dances an improbable Jerk with Anne of the bare shoulders. Joss is mixing the Cry with some rhythm that makes it impossible to do otherwise. Marc tries to look cool. He looks preposterous. Have you ever noticed how people who are afraid of looking a fool are more likely than others to do so?

Fab and Irène go through the burnished sea spray haloing the dawn.

'Tonight,' says Fab, 'something's happened to us. *We have become one with the speakers.*'

And there's nothing virtual about it. The night offers only two options, Fab off his face and Joss.

Despite the agonising Cry unleashing mass hysteria all around them, Anne and Marc have come closer together. They have been engaged in wordless conversation. When she snuggles up against him, he does the same.

# 5.00 A.M.

Why live when you can get yourself buried for only ten bucks?

American advertising slogan

Slowly but surely, five o'clock has reluctantly come around.

Boredom breaks on the horizon with its disappointed yawns. It is the emollient hour, the hour of turpitude. Couples and livers have been serenely self-destructing; now it is time to put on a brave face. At 5 a.m. all that remains in a nightclub are the apoplectic losers and indolent idiots who know that whatever may happen, they have little chance of getting anything up. You can see them dragging their feet, glass in hand, a little stooped. The club-men turn in circles, like vultures in search of pretty girls turned ugly.

Anne alone sparkles, her blue eyes right in the middle. Marc decides to give her a baby right here and now.

'First one to come has to bring the other breakfast in bed tomorrow.'

He leads her to the toilets. And, astonishingly, she follows.

He opens the door to the ladies' toilets and immediately shuts it again, begging Anne not to go inside. What he has discovered is so indescribable that it is best to describe it without delay. It begins with the stench of melted wax, warm blood and fresh bile. Then he opens his eyes only to feel the urgent need to close them again. Next, he reopens his eyes and looks, for he always wants to SEE. That is all he knows how to do, SEE. It was something he learned early. And, let's be honest, the more unendurable the sight, the more it pleases him to stare.

The photographer, Ondine Quinsac, is still alive, crucified to a door, her belly covered with a network of thin, bloated, blood-streaked ridges, like discarded orange peel. A cigarette has been stubbed out in her belly button. The lacerated breasts of Solange Justerini have been used as pincushions. She is still breathing through the zip-mouth of her gimp mask. The shaven genitalia of the unconscious press attaché is stuffed with a handful of lit burning candles as in the 148th murderous passion of the *120 Days of Sodom*. The torture of the three guests is the work of someone literate. They moan – it must be a strange feeling, such pain inflicted of one's own free will – just beside a talking condom dispenser which intones: 'Did-you-re-mem-ber-your-BRONX-lu-bri-cant? Don't-for-get-va-se-line-da-ma-ges-la-tex.'

In front of Ondine's mouth is a small wireless microphone attached to a headset, into which she whispers:

'Thank you Joss thank you thank you enough no stop.'

The sound is being broadcast live into the hall. A DAT walkman lying on the toilet paper is feeding directly into the HF of the sound system.

The Cry which has been making Shit dance is the stunned torture of three girls on Digital Audio Tape. Joss planned his scheme down to the last detail, Marc realises this fact in an instant, he realises that he had no idea what was going on from the very beginning, he realises that God hates back rooms.

The music goes on No Ah No Ah Noooo Not That Beep Beep Beep Boom Boom Tudi Tudi Zzzza. The Larsen effect. A 140BPM morning. Not all auroras are borealis.

*

It is at this very moment in this very place that Marc takes the finest Polaroid of his career. In the minute that follows, his beard grows back.

Then Joss Dumoulin walks out of the cubicle, unsteady with fatigue. He has probably taken tranquillisers. He's sweating Lexomil. Unless maybe it's Rohypnol. Don't shoot the DJ: he has already entered REM sleep. The lighting flares and the speakers implode. The eardrums are long gone. It's not now, it's when. Josh is shivering feverishly.

'Mmgrrllbbmrrr I feel weak, I'm out of whack, I'm a slug, hi Anne, hi Marc, God you're so fucking lucky Marronnier, must remember to get my brain checked, and where the hell is Clio? And what's the next record? My head's spinning and I've got knots in my stomach, God, come-down's a bitch, when is this antidepressant going to kick in? I should get some sleep, just a month or two in a hammock, but we're all so alone on this earth, it's appalling ... Okay, you need to think about something else, breathe deeply, think happy thoughts, this synthetic angst is terrible, it's just the drugs making you think ... So alone, got no one, NO ONE ... All these strangers, what do they know? Who here is gonna love me? Just keep the eyes open, relax the jaw, drink some water, yeah, a glass of water, quick. But what? Why are you looking at me like that?'

Marc and Anne stare at Joss as, trembling, whip in hand, he drinks from the tap. They stare at him and stare at him and then, nauseous, walk out. Joss yells after them:

'What? What's the matter? They're the ones who started it, the sluts. I can do what the fuck I like! I'm JOSS DUMOULIN, shit! I've every right! You don't know what it's like, being JOSS DUMOULIN, it means you've got NO FUCKING PRIVATE

LIFE! I'm famous all over the world! Everyone loves me! I'm so fucking lonely!'

His shrieking is lost in the confusion, dying away as Anne and Marc climb the stairs to the exit.

Alone before his three victims, Joss falls to his knees and murmurs:

'I'm famous ... Hey, tell them, girls, tell them you'd do anything for me, anything ... I'm still an ordinary guy, tell them! I'm not big-headed, am I ... I'll give you a thousand bucks each ...'

The seconds die like minutes in groups of sixty. The only thing awake is his gastritis. Sometimes he can stay for ten minutes without blinking, his eyes sting. Sometimes he can stay for ten minutes with his eyes closed, and they sting all the more. He puts on his WWI gas mask.

Joss, all alone, all night long.

In a three-quarter shot, the camera films him on all fours, wheezing like an asthmatic; the gas mask and the headset make him into a giant insect. It is almost impossible to hear what he's muttering, but listen closely and over the moaning of the three women, it sounds as if Joss is drooling.

Dolly out to a flick-pan and track across the dance floor filled with insensate dancers, POV low-angle tracking shot mounting the stairs, POV 5 inches to a two-shot of Marc Marronnier standing in the doorway, he is writing his review without pausing to recover his breath while Anne gets her coat from the cloakroom.

No, it's not the title of the new San-Antonio thriller. You'll just have to get used to it: the club that everyone will be talking about this winter bears a name which sanctions the most puerile schoolboy humour. The place de la Madeleine may never recover.

Last night, a privileged few were resurrected to the land of the living. Our dear friend **Loulou Zibeline**, radiant as ever, provided the *bons mots*. Gifted young designer **Irène de Kazatchok** spent the evening in the company of famed presenter **Fab**, whose outfit shocked more than one guest (see photo of **Ondine Quinsac**)!

In this novel post-modern setting, decorated in the form of a giant public toilet, **Joss Dumoulin** (a DJ who needs no intro-duction) brought together the *crème de la crème* for a stunning one-nighter: **the Hardissons**, both in attendance, had to bring a babysitter for their newborn; supermodel **Clio**, with her inim-itable flair, wore a stunningly sexy little number (in fact the ebullient producer Robert de Dax was quite captivated by her, although he arrived accompanied by his new protégée **Solange Justerini**!); as for **Jean-Georges Parmentier**, yet again he bent over backwards to liven things up . . .

Towards the close of the evening, following a sumptuous dinner, we were treated to a number of entertaining surprise guests: a concert by the rising stars Fuck Yo Mama, followed by a gargantuan bubble bath which – pardon the pun – plunged everyone into a state of euphoria!

**SHIT**, place de la Madeleine, 75008 Paris.

Marc puts the cap back on his pen before kissing Anne. Tomorrow, this scrap of paper will earn him 1,000 francs. Barely enough to cover his dry-cleaning bill.

# 6.00 A.M.

'That's your response to everything: drink?'
'No, that's my response to nothing.'

Charles Bukowski

Anne and Marc take French leave. There's no one dancing any more. Outside the door, they stumble over a number of jellyfish in humanoid form. In the stairwell, they say goodbye to Donald Suldiras whose wing collar is stained with blood. Ali de Hirschenberg is carrying a candlestick and Baron von Meinerhof is playing with his riding-crop. Joss's friends rush towards the exit, chain-smoking cigarettes. Push-up bras hang from the great crystal chandelier.

They tip the cloakroom attendant ten francs and give the old woman lying on the footpath outside 500.

At Shit, the only remaining survivors begin a penultimate round, break into one last chorus, rebuff the punishing dawn, in short they hold back the night make-it-last-at-least-until-forever.

No longer will they trample the bodies of their friends. No longer will they capsize on rooftops. Where are the undrinkable cocktails? The *décolletés* which flutter open at just the right moment, the somnambulistic music, the obscure lighting, the show-offs showing off, the drunken policemen, the emaciated guy threatening them with his dirty hypodermic? They will survive. They stagger along the road. They will die much later, with a minimum of fuss. The world is almost lavish. And the day purrs with promise.

All in all, the world has not stopped turning.

They bump into Fab and Irène. She tells them that in the States there's a word for people like them: 'Eurotrash'.

Passers-by are on their way to work. The mouths of the metro vomit up bunches of bureaucrats. A glazier is repairing the windows at Ralph Lauren. The shutters are coming up at Fauchon.

Marc dreams of a virtual evening, an event which would not actually take place. The guest list would be posted at the entrance, and reading it, guests would be able to imagine what MIGHT HAVE BEEN. Each would concoct his or her own tale. A virtual evening is the perfect evening, an out of focus film. Silent noise. During a virtual evening, no one risks anything. In a virtual evening, Anne would not presently be shivering with cold and Marc would not have the urge to weep pleonastically like Mary Magdalene on the *place* that bears her name. ('One day,' he thinks, 'the place should be renamed the "place Marcel Proust".')

Suddenly, everything is clear. He remembers. He looks like a right muppet. Anne's face, which he is sure he's seen somewhere before, is the face of the woman he married two years ago. The drunkenness threw him off balance: Marc has spent the whole evening searching for something he had all the time.

Joy is a simple thing. The day breaks, you hold someone's hand in yours. You walk. You breathe. You are grateful, but to whom? Sometimes happiness seems inevitable. Suddenly, in his head, Marc hears phrases like: 'Love can save the world.'

*

Of course he's married: and he married for love, to boot. Marc loves unfashionable pleasures. A handsome young married couple trudge their way through the eighth *arrondissement*, an incongruous sight, as if they were terrorists. Except that in their shoes, a member of Action Directe would not hold out for long. Too bad: they think of themselves as post-modern adventurers: they add tarragon to lamb chops. They eat overripe camembert and help themselves to another glass of burgundy. Their glasses get lost under the bed. Love is a punnet of radishes bought from Tarascon and eaten with a pinch of sea salt on a park bench. They have simultaneous orgasms. They find their glasses under the bed. They always brush their teeth. They make every effort so that this miracle will endure.

'I think I did the right thing, marrying you,' says Anne, pretty as a pear-drop.

'If you hadn't, I'd be terminally dead,' says Marc. 'Why did you come to Shit? Were you spying on me?'

'Just making sure that you were propping up the bar, feeling sorry for yourself. Once again you spent the whole night cheating on me with yourself.'

Marc takes advantage of the situation to grope her. Since they're married, he thinks such things are normal – in case of grievance, he can always produce a marriage certificate duly signed and sealed. The laws of the Republic are on his side.

Shortly afterwards, in the taxi, Anne says:

'In New York, taxis are yellow, in London, they're black, in Paris, they're shit.'

'Why do you pay a taxi at the end? You should pay them at the beginning.'

'Blind trust. We just give them an address and naively they take us there.'

'Yeah, but they have no guarantee that we'll pay the fare.'

'When you get there, the driver turns and looks at you like a dumb animal, as if he's just realised that he's asking for money we could very well hang on to by doing a runner.'

'That'll be sixty francs, please,' says the driver, turning a little worriedly, as they have just arrived.

Why look on the day? It gives off too much light. Eyes dazzled by the pale sky no longer recognise anything. Birds fly, dogs bark, lovers wend their way home. The holiday in a coma wakes to the light of day. The morning is yellow as a cheese omelette.

It's not difficult to leave the eighth *arrondissement*. Their souls hold hands. They run: today is another day. Perhaps they're sleepwalking, too lazy to be genuine cheats. Marc is starving, but already he knows that he couldn't eat a thing. He doesn't even have a headache any more. He will be deprived of his hangover.

Tomorrow is a kiss on the back of the neck. Tomorrow is the mist on your forehead. Tomorrow is a laddered stocking, a bra strap. Tomorrow is the day of eternal first day of Lent. Tomorrow the night will end in silence. Someone will beat it to death with a baseball bat. For the first time in his life, Marc accepts that he is *normal*. And of course, the consequence of pretending to be in love is that in the end, you are.

They are the moral of this immoral tale. The rest is nothing but literature.

Marc never saw Joss Dumoulin again. Sometimes he even wonders whether Joss ever existed.

# 7.00 A.M.

The cab is a pillow,
the streets are blankets,
the dawn is my bed.

Richard Brautigan
'Day for Night'

And so Anne Marronnier brought her husband back home. As they were going to bed, he had the last word:

'The sun also rises; me neither.'

The Lusitanian chambermaid's vacuum cleaner serves as their alarm clock.

*Verbier 1991–1993*

# LOVE LASTS THREE YEARS

*For*
*Christine de Chasteigner and Jean-Michel Beigbeder,*
*without whom neither this book (nor I)*
*would have seen the light of day.*

I speak with the authority of failure.

F. Scott Fitzgerald

What?! It's the truth! There's no point pretending. Tell it like it is. You love someone and then you don't.

Françoise Sagan
*(during a dinner with Brigitte Bardot and Bernard Franck at her home in 1966)*

# I

# CONNECTED VESSELS

CONSEQUENCES

# I

# Endless Love

Love is a battle which is lost before it is begun.

In the beginning, everything is wonderful, even you are wonderful. You can't believe you're so much in love. Each new day brings with it some small new miracle. No one on earth has ever known the love you share. Suddenly, you know that happiness truly exists, and it is simple: it is her face. The universe smiles down on you. In that first year, life is an endless procession of sunny mornings, even on snowy afternoons. You write books about it. You get married as soon as possible – when you're this happy, why stop to think? Thinking just makes people sad; life is all that matters.

In the second year, things change. You become closer. You're proud of the intimacy you share. You know what your wife is thinking without her ever having to say a word. It is bliss to be one flesh. When you go out together, people sometimes take you for brother and sister. You feel flattered, but the comparison begins to take its toll. You make love less and less frequently and you think it doesn't matter. You think that with every passing day your love grows stronger when in fact the end is nigh. You stick up for marriage when your single friends tell you they hardly recognise you. As you trot out this speech you've learned off by heart, making sure not to stare at the pretty girls who light up the street, you hardly recognise yourself.

In the third year, you no longer restrain yourself from staring at the pretty young girls who light up the street. You and your wife barely speak these days. When you go out to dinner as a couple, you spend hours listening to the people at the next table. You go out all the time now: it gives you an excuse not to have sex. Before you know it, you can't stand the sight of your wife any more, which is hardly surprising, since you're already in love with someone else. There is only one point on which you were right all along: life is for living. The third year brings good news and bad. The good news is your wife has had enough and she walks out, the bad news is you're writing a book about it.

# II

# The Gay Divorcé

The art of drunk-driving is to aim for the space between the buildings. Marc Marronnier cranks the accelerator, thereby forcing his moped to go faster. He careens between cars which flash their headlights and beep their horns as he rubs up against their bodywork, like a redneck at a wedding. This is ironic since Marc Marronnier is celebrating his divorce. Tonight, he's doing the Double-5 Tour. He's already running late: hitting five clubs in one night (Castel–Buddha–Bus–Cabaret–Queen) is tough enough, so you can imagine how difficult it is to do a Double-5, which means hitting each club twice in one night.

Marc often goes out alone. The urban male is usually a loner wandering through a world of vague acquaintances, who reassure each other with bone-crushing handshakes. Every kiss on the cheek is a trophy. The urban male gives the impression of being a high-flyer, by greeting famous people when in fact he is unemployed. He frequents bars and clubs where the music is just loud enough to make conversation impossible. God created partying so that the urban male would not have to think. There are few men as well connected as Marc Marronnier, and few who are as lonely.

But tonight is not some random party, tonight is Marc's divorce party! He began his evening by buying a bottle of hard liquor in each club and has been making steady progress on each of them.

Tonight, Marc Marronnier, you are King of the Night! Beloved of everyone, club owners kiss you on the lips, you jump every queue, always get the best table, never forget a name, laugh at everyone's jokes (particularly when they're not funny), people give you drugs for free, you appear in photos in every glossy magazine. In a few short years in the gossip columns, you've come a long way. You are a prince among men! The Urban Alpha Male. So, tell me something, why exactly did your wife leave you?

'It was a mutual thing on her part,' Marc mutters, staggering into Le Bus. The he adds:

'I married Anne because she was an angel, which is precisely why we got divorced. I thought I was looking for love, until one day I realised that what I was looking for was a way out.'

He changes the subject.

'Wow!' he shouts. 'The girls in here are pretty decent. I should have brushed my teeth. Mademoiselle, you are ravishing, may I remove your clothing, please?'

In his soft velvet suit, Marc Marronnier pretends to be a chauvinist bastard, because he's ashamed of the fact that he's soft-hearted. Marc has just turned thirty: the awkward age when you're too old to be young and too young to be old. He does his best to live down to his reputation. He wouldn't want to disappoint people. He's spent so long trying to live up to his image that he's become a caricature. Bored of trying to prove that he's a profound, compassionate man, he pretends to be a superficial prick by behaving as outrageously – some would say pathetically – as possible. So he only has himself to blame if, when he howls from the dance floor 'Way hey! I'm divorced!', no one comes to comfort him. Only the laserbeams which pierce his heart like so many swords.

All too soon it's time to perform the difficult manoeuvre of putting one foot in front of the other. Marc lurches onto his scooter. It's freezing. Marc feels tears streak his face as he speeds through the city. It must be the wind. He is completely emotionless. He's not wearing a crash-helmet. *La dolce vita*? What *dolce vita*? He has too many memories, too many things he needs to forget. Forgetting is hard work, he will have to live so many precious moments to replace these memories.

He hooks up with his friends at Le Baron, a brothel on the avenue Marceau. The champagne is pricey and so are the girls. I mean, it's 6,000 francs if you want a threesome, but it's only 3,000 francs for one girl. They don't do discounts for bulk buyers. The girls insist he pay cash so Marc goes out to an ATM. They head off to a hotel, the girls strip off in the taxi and go down on him simultaneously, Marc leans on their heads for balance. In the hotel room, they slather themselves with scented cream, he fucks one girl while she goes down on the other. When he realises he won't be able to come, he fakes an orgasm and rushes into the bathroom where he carefully dumps the empty condom in the bin.

On his way home in the taxi, he hears Christophe singing 'Le Beau Bizarre':

> The champagne flute
> That's bitter like bile
> And a band wearing sharp suits
> Just out of style
> Plays the silence of my life
> Deserted a while.

He decides that from now on he'll have a wank if he's going out, that way he won't be tempted to do something stupid.

# III

# On the Beach

I'd like to introduce myself. I'm the author and I'd like to welcome you all to my brain. Sorry for interrupting your reading. No more cheating: I've decided to be my own central character.

Usually, nothing much happens in my life. My loved ones don't die, I've never set foot in Sarajevo. My tribulations are usually played out in restaurants and nightclubs and elegant apartments with ornamental mouldings. The most depressing thing to happen to me recently was not getting an invite to John Galliano's show. And now, suddenly, I find myself consumed by grief.

There was a phase when all my friends were alcoholics, then they were all druggies, then there was the phase when they all got married, right now they're going through the one where they all get divorced before they die. Curiously, all this happens in jaunty places like the one I'm in now: La Voile Rouge, a sun-drenched beach in Saint-Tropez, where they play eurodance in the bars and spray Louis Roederer Cristal over bikini-clad lumpensluts only to lick it out of their belly buttons. Here, I'm deafened by the sound of forced laughter. I'd throw myself into the sea and drown if there weren't so many jet-skis.

How can I have allowed appearances to rule my life? People

are always saying 'You have to keep up appearances'. I think you should gun them down. It's the only way to survive.

# IV

# The Saddest Human Being I Ever Met

In the depths of the Paris winter, some places are colder than others. In the bars, no matter how much vodka you drink, it feels like there's a blizzard blowing. The ice age has come early. Even crowds make me shiver.

Where did I go wrong? I did all the right things: I was born into a family of good social standing, I went to the best schools, the Lycée Montaigne and the Lycée Louis-le-Grand, I went to a good university where I met clever people, went clubbing with them, some of them even went so far as to offer me a job, I married the prettiest girl I knew. Why is it so cold in here? Where did I go wrong? I always behaved myself, always tried to make other people happy. So why don't I get to be happy too? Why did the uncomplicated joy they dangled in front of me turn out to be a complicated misery?

I am a dead man. Every morning, I wake up with an unbearable longing to go to sleep. I wear black because I am in mourning for my life. I wear widow's weeds for the man I might have been. With heavy tread, I pace the rue des Beaux-Arts, the street where, like me, Oscar Wilde died. I wander into restaurants but never eat. Head waiters look on furiously as I ignore the dishes placed before me. But how many dead people do you know who wolf down the *specialité du chef* and lick their lips? This means that I'm constantly drinking on an empty stomach. The advantage of this is that I get drunk more quickly. The disadvantage is that I've now got a stomach ulcer.

I don't smile any more. It's too much for me. I'm dead and buried. I'll never have children. Dead men don't procreate. I'm a dead man who goes round shaking hands with people in cafés. I'm a friendly corpse as corpses go, but I can't stand the cold. I think I am the saddest human being I've ever met.

In the depths of the Paris winter, when the thermometer dips below zero, the human animal needs a bright, cosy bar to shelter in at night. There, protected by the herd, he can allow himself to shiver.

# V

# Best Before Date

You can be the strong, silent type and still cry like a baby. All it takes is for you to find out that love lasts three years. It's a revelation I wouldn't wish on my worst enemy – a rhetorical expression, since I haven't got one. Snobs don't have enemies. They spend their time slandering other people in the hope that they might get some.

The life of a mayfly lasts only a day, a rose, three days. A cat may live for thirteen years, love lasts for three. It's a simple fact. First, a year of passion, then a year of intimacy, lastly a year of boredom.

In year one, you say: 'If you leave me, I'LL KILL MYSELF.'

In year two, you say: 'If you leave me, I'll be hurt, but I'll survive.'

In year three, you say: 'If you leave me, I'll break out the champagne.'

No one warns you that love lasts three years. The myth of romance is founded on this carefully guarded secret. People let you believe that love is for life when, chemically speaking, love evaporates after three years. I read it in a woman's magazine: love is a fleeting series of bursts of dopamine, noradrenalin and oxytocin. A tiny molecule named phenylethylamine (PEA)

176

creates feelings of joy, bliss and euphoria. When neurones in the limbic system are suddenly flooded with PEA, we call it love at first sight. Intimacy is based on endorphins (the opium of the couple). Society deliberately sets out to sell you the idea that love lasts forever when it's scientifically proven that, after three years, the hormones stop working.

The statistics speak for themselves: on average, passion lasts for 317.5 days (I've always wondered what happens during that last half-day . . .); two out of three relationships end in divorce and within three years of marriage. Since 1947, the United Nations has published a survey of the incidence of divorce in seventy-two countries which states that the majority of divorces occur in the fourth year of marriage (meaning one of the partners filed for divorce in year three). 'From Finland and Russia, to Egypt and South Africa, hundreds of millions of people – men and women who speak different languages, have different jobs, different tastes, different currencies, whisper different prayers and fear different devils – people who nurture an infinite diversity of hopes and dreams have one thing in common: they are more likely to get divorced after three years of living together.' The banality of divorce is just one more humiliation.

Three years! In statistics, in biochemistry and in my own experience, the duration of love is identical. A disturbing co-incidence. Why three years and not two, or four, or six hundred? To my mind, this research simply confirms the validity of the three stages of love as defined by Stendhal, Roland Barthes and Barbara Cartland: passion–intimacy–boredom, a cycle in which each stage lasts precisely one year – a triad as sacred as the Holy Trinity.

In year one, you buy furniture.

In year two, you move furniture around.

In year three, you argue over who gets the furniture.

Leo Ferré's song says it all: '*Avec le temps, on n'aime plus*'. How can you possibly argue with glands and neurotransmitters that will let you down as soon as the time comes? I suppose you could try lyric poetry, but faced with the twin forces of science and statistics, poetry is doomed from the start.

# VI

# The End of the Road

I got home shit-faced. Getting shit-faced at my age is embarrassing. Getting hammered every night when you're eighteen is all very well, when you're thirty, it's pathetic. I took half a tab of E so I could snog a couple of girls I didn't know. Without the E, I'd never have got up the nerve. The number of girls I didn't kiss because I was afraid of getting knocked back is incalculable. That's what makes me charming, apparently; I'm not aware of it. At Le Queen, two gorgeous drunk blondes whose tongues in my ears were creating a surround sound gurgling effect asked me:

'Your place or ours?'

After I'd given them a quick three-way snog (and nibbled each of their four breasts), I answered proudly:

'You're going to your place and I'm heading back to mine. I haven't got any condoms and anyway, tonight I'm celebrating my divorce so I'd be so nervous I wouldn't be able to get it up.'

A scooter ride later, I arrived back in my empty flat. I could feel the hand of dread crushing my stomach: I was coming down from the ecstasy. That was something I didn't need: there's no point spending the whole night avoiding reality only to catch up with it when you get home. I found a wrap with a little bit of coke in the pocket of my jacket. I practically snorted the paper with it. That should soften the come-down. There's a dab of coke on the tip of my nose. I don't feel tired any more. The sun is already climbing into the sky and the adult male population are heading to work while a retarded teenager isn't planning on getting up for hours. I'm too tripped out to sleep, read or write, so I stare at the ceiling and grind my teeth. With my red face and my white nose, in the mirror I look like a clown the wrong way round.

I decide to give work a miss today. I'm chuffed with myself for turning down a bisexual orgy the day after my divorce. I'm tired of sleeping with girls I hate waking up with.

Apart from a saucepan of milk boiling over, there aren't many things on earth as miserable as I am.

# VII

# Some Tips for Surviving Heartbreak

Repeat the following phrases regularly:

1) THERE'S NO SUCH THING AS HAPPINESS
2) I'LL NEVER FIND TRUE LOVE
3) NOTHING MATTERS

I'm not kidding, it might sound stupid but when I was depressed, those three tips probably saved my life. Try them next time you're having a breakdown. I highly recommend it.

I'm also including a list of depressing songs you can listen to to help you get back on your feet again: 'April, Come She Will', Simon & Garfunkel (x 20), 'Trouble', Cat Stevens (x 10), 'Something in the Way She Moves', James Taylor (x 10), 'Et si tu n'existais pas', Joey Dassin (x 5), 'Sixty Years On' back to back with 'Border Song', Elton John (x 40), 'Everybody Hurts', R.E.M. (x 5), 'Quelques mots d'amour', Michel Berger (x 40 but don't brag about it), 'Memory Motel', Rolling Stones (x 8½), 'Living Without You', Randy Newman (x 100), 'Caroline No', The Beach Boys (x 600), the 'Kreutzer' Sonata, Ludwig van Beethoven (x 6,000). It's a great idea for a compilation CD – I've already got the slogan:

'Songs for the Dumped:

Love Songs to Bum You Out.'

# VIII

# For Those Who Missed the Beginning

I'm thirty years old and still unable to look at a pretty girl without blushing. It's upsetting being so sensitive. I'm too apathetic to truly fall in love, but too sensitive to be really indifferent. In other words, too feeble to stay married. What's got into me? I'm tempted to suggest that you read volumes one and two of this trilogy, but that wouldn't be fair since the aforementioned masterpieces were remaindered shortly after their critical success. So I'll recapitulate: I was a shameless clubber, the perfect product of the consumer society. I was born twenty years after the liberation of Auschwitz, on 21 September 1965, the first day of autumn. I came into the world just as the autumn leaves were falling, as the days were getting shorter. Maybe this explains why I'm so disillusioned. I used to earn a living stringing words together for magazines and ad agencies – advertising, I discovered, has the advantage of paying more money for fewer words. I made a name for myself organising events in Paris back when no one organised events in Paris. It's completely unrelated to my work as a wordsmith, but that's how I became famous. Which just goes to show that these days writers are much less important than people who get their picture in the gossip columns.

I surprised my potential biographers when I fell in love and married. One day, I thought I caught a glimpse of eternity in a pair of blue eyes. Having spent my whole life flitting from party to party, job to job, terrified that if I stopped I would be miserable, now suddenly I thought I was happy.

Anne, my wife, had an unreal, a luminous, almost ethereal beauty. She was much too beautiful to be happy, but that was something I didn't find out until it was too late. I used to gaze at her for hours. Sometimes she'd catch me and snap: 'Stop staring, you're embarrassing me.' But watching her go about her life had become my favourite show. Guys like me who grew up thinking they were ugly are usually so stunned when they manage to seduce a pretty girl that they have to pop the question almost immediately.

The next bit is hardly terribly original: let's just say we moved into an apartment too small for the immense love we shared. As a result, we spent too much time going out. It became a vicious circle. People would say: 'They're always going out, those two.'

'Yeah . . . there must be trouble at home.'

And maybe they were right, though they were quite happy to have a beautiful woman at one of their shabby little parties for once.

Life being what it is, as soon as you've had a taste of happiness, it kicks you in the balls.

We took it in turns to be unfaithful.

We broke up the same way we got together: without knowing why.

Marriage is a put-up job, a scam, a calculated con, it sucks you in and spits you out. How? I'll tell you how. A guy asks a girl to marry him. He's so scared he's shitting himself. It's touching, really; there he is, blushing and sweating and stammering. The girl laughs nervously, her eyes shining, and asks him to repeat the question. But from the moment she says 'yes', both of them are suddenly lumbered with the longest 'to do' list in the world: dinner with bride's family, lunch with groom's family, seating arrangements, dress fitting, stand-up rows, no burping or farting in front of the in-laws, stand up straight and smile, smile, smile. It's a nightmare, and the wedding is just the beginning: afterwards, as we shall see, everything conspires to ensure our lovers come to despise one another.

# IX

# Rain over Copacabana

Fairy-tale romances only happen in fairy tales. Reality never quite lives up to the hype. The truth is always a disappointment, which is why everybody lies.

The truth is a photo of another woman accidentally turning up in my carry-on bag on New Year's Eve in Rio de Janeiro (Brazil). The truth is that love starts out all hearts and flowers and ends up all livers and weeds. Looking for her toothbrush, Anne was taken aback to find a Polaroid and a handful of love-letters from someone else.

Anne dumped me there at the airport in Rio. She told me she was going back to Paris on her own. I was hardly in a position to argue. She stood dumbfounded, sobbing. Desolate as a woman who has seen her world crumble in a matter of seconds. A soft-hearted girl who suddenly discovers that life is cruel, that her marriage is falling apart. She was blinded by grief: there was no airport, no queue, no arrivals' board, everything had disappeared – everything except me, the man who had betrayed her. I wish now that I'd put my arms around her, but I felt uncomfortable because she wouldn't stop crying, because everyone was staring at me. Being shown up in public as a bastard is embarrassing enough.

I didn't beg her forgiveness, I said: 'You'd better hurry or you'll miss your plane.' I didn't lift a finger to save her. Even now when I remember what I did, my oversized chin trembles. She stared at me, her eyes imploring, sad, tearful, hateful, care-worn, anxious, disillusioned, innocent, proud, contemptuous and yet somehow still the same blue they had always been. I knew then that I would never forget the pain in her eyes at that moment. It was just one thing I'd have to learn to live with. Everyone always sympathises with the person who gets hurt, no one gives a toss about the one doing the hurting. You just have to take it on the chin. As Benjamin Constant writes at the end of *Adolphe*: 'The great question in life is the suffering we cause, and the most ingenious metaphysics do not justify the man who has broken the heart that loved him.'

After Anne went home, I moped around Copacabana on my own. Feeling more abandoned than any man has ever been, I drank twenty caipirinhas. I felt like a bastard, a shit, a monster. That year it rained over Rio on New Year's Eve for the first time in decades. Divine retribution. As I knelt on the midnight beach amid the deafening throb of the samba, I too began to rain.

There are nights when you would give anything in the world to be able to sleep. To sleep so you might wake up from this nightmare. Nights when you wish none of this had ever happened. When you want to press Command-Z and undo your whole life. Because you hurt yourself more than anyone else when you make someone suffer.

I remember the night when I first tasted insomnia. A million Brazilians dressed in white stood on Copacabana beach, in the rain, watching the fireworks' display in front of the Méridien Hotel. According to tradition, if you toss a white flower into the sea on New Year's Eve and make a wish, the gods will grant that wish in the New Year. I threw a huge bouquet of flowers into the waves and wished as hard as I could for everything to turn out all right. I don't know what happened: maybe my flowers weren't pretty enough, maybe the gods weren't listening, but I never got my wish.

# X

# Palais de Justice, Paris

Divorce is not something to be entered into lightly. What kind of people have we become if we treat it as a less than solemn act? Anne had had faith in me. She had entrusted her life to me before God (and, more importantly, the French Republic). I had signed a contract in which I promised to spend my life caring for her, raising our children. And I had deceived her. It was Anne who filed for divorce: it was her turn, after all I was the one who asked her to marry me. We would never have any children now, which was just as well for the kids. Having a coward and a deserter for a father is a lot for a kid to deal with. I blame myself, that way I don't have to blame someone else.

Why does no one come to a divorce? When we got married, I had all my friends around me; on the day we got divorced, I was unbelievably alone. There were no witnesses, no maids of honour, no family, no drunken mates to slap me on the back. No flowers by request. I wanted someone to throw something, maybe not confetti but, I don't know, rotten tomatoes. I mean, chucking things at people on the steps of the Palais de Justice is hardly unusual. So where were all my dearest friends – they were happy enough to pig out on petits fours at my wedding, why was it they wouldn't come within a mile of my divorce? I think things should be the other way round – you should get married in private and have your friends round for the divorce.

There are Church of England vicars, apparently, who organise pleasant little ceremonies where the divorce is consummated by the forswearing of vows and the returning of rings.

'I give back this ring as a sign of our divorce.' As a concept, I think it's got style. The Pope should look into it: it would put bums on seats, and they'd make more money selling off wedding rings than they get from the collection plate. This is what I'm thinking about as the judge is trying to reconcile us. He asks if we're really sure that we want to get a divorce. He's talking to us like we're four years old. I feel like saying 'no, actually, we're only here for the beer'. And then I realise that he's seen right through us: we are four-year-olds.

Divorce is the moment when a man loses his intellectual virginity. Now that we don't have 'a good war' to make men of us, it is domestic tragedies (losing your father or your mother, waking up to find yourself paralysed after a car accident or losing your home after an unfair dismissal) that force us to grow up.

. . . Or maybe adultery made a man of me?

We all pretend we don't care about getting divorced, but sooner or later you realise that somehow you've gone from *Love Story* to *Kramer vs. Kramer*. Forget all the memories you cherished, forget the cute little pet names you made up for each other, burn the photos of your honeymoon, turn off the radio when they play 'our song'. Suddenly, commonplace phrases like 'How do I look in this?' or 'What do you fancy doing tonight?' can have you in tears because they bring back terrible memories. Suddenly, inexplicably, you find yourself weeping every time you see a couple reunited at an airport. Even the Song of Songs is torture: 'Thy cheeks are comely with rows of jewels, thy neck with chains of gold . . . Thou hast ravished my heart, my sister, my spouse; thou hast ravished my heart with one of thine eyes, with one chain of thy neck.'

Anne and I will meet only once more, in the presence of a lawyer with a fixed grin who, to make matters worse, has the temerity to be nine months pregnant. We will kiss each other like old friends when we arrive. Afterwards, we'll go for coffee together and pretend the world hasn't come to an end. Around us, people will be going on with their lives. We'll chat good-naturedly and when we go our separate ways, though a passer-by would notice nothing strange, it will be forever. 'See you,' will be the last lie we will ever tell each other.

# XI

# The Human Man at Thirty

Where I come from, no one has second thoughts before they turn thirty, by which time, of course, it's too late to have first thoughts.

It goes like this: you turn twenty, you have a bit of a laugh and when you wake up, you're thirty. It's all over: never again will you have a birthday that begins with a '2'. Suddenly, you're ten years older than you were a decade ago and ten kilos heavier than you were last year. How much time have you got left? Ten years? Twenty? Thirty? Average life expectancy suggests you have forty-two years left, if you're a man; fifty, if you're a woman. But that's without taking illness, baldness, senility and liver spots into account. Nobody ever thinks to ask: Have I made the most of things? Should I have done things differently? Am I with the right person, in the right place? What has life got to offer me? From the moment we're born to the moment we die, we're on autopilot, and it requires superhuman strength to change course.

When I was twenty, I thought I knew everything there was to know. By thirty, I realised I didn't know shit. I had spent ten years learning things that I would then spend ten years having to unlearn.

The problem for Anne and me was that we made the perfect couple. Never trust a perfect couple: they're too busy looking good, too busy strutting around with forced smiles like they're promoting a film at Cannes. The problem with marrying someone you love is that everything is perfect from the start. The only possible surprise in a marriage like that is a catastrophe. If there are no catastrophes, then what? You trundle on together until you die and wind up in heaven without ever having lived. For that to happen, you would have to live out your whole life in a perfect movie, with the same perfect cast. It's impossible. When you've got everything you ever wanted, you wind up hoping things will fuck up just so you can be free. You pray for a catastrophe to come and ease your pain.

People don't get married for themselves. It was a long time before I could admit that the reason I got married was all about other people. You get married to piss off your friends or make your parents happy, often both and sometimes the other way round. These days, ninety per cent of posh weddings are just social events which make it possible for your over-anxious parents to invite the overanxious parents who invited them last year. Sometimes, your prospective in-laws may check to see whether their future son-in-law is listed in *Who's Who*, have the engagement ring weighed to calculate the carats or insist on selling the photos to *Hello!* But that's a worst case scenario.

You get married for the same reason you take your finals or get your driving licence: you do it to be like everyone else, because you're desperate to prove that you're normal, normal, NORMAL. If you can't be better than everyone else, you try to prove you're just like everyone else, because you're terrified they might be better than you. And this is the perfect way to sabotage your relationship.

But middle-class moralists are not the only ones endorsing marriage. It is a massive act of collective brainwashing; advertisers, film-makers, journalists and even novelists endeavour to convince every little girl that what she really, really wants is a big white dress and a ring on her finger when without all the propaganda, the idea of marriage would never have occurred to her. Oh, she would have dreamed of love – the emotional roller-coaster that is True Love – otherwise what would be the point of living? But the idea of marriage, the Institution-Which-Makes-Love-Tedious, what Maupassant called 'the ball and chain of endless love and lifelong commitment', would never enter her head. In an ideal world, a twenty-year-old girl would be repelled by such an artificial concept. She would yearn for sincerity, for passion, for unconditional love – not some guy in a rented tuxedo. She would yearn for a man who could offer her a lifetime of surprises, not some bloke who could offer her flat-pack Ikea furniture. She would let nature – by which we mean desire – take its course.

Sadly, frustrated mothers dream that one day their daughters will know the same unhappiness they have known; and sadly their daughters have spent too much time watching soap operas. And so they wait for Mr Right – a pathetic marketing concept destined to turns girls into bitter, disillusioned old maids – when only Mr Right Now can truly make them happy.

Of course, the aristocracy says things are different nowadays, times have changed, but take the word of a frustrated victim: intimidation has never been more brutal than it is today in this world of illusory freedom. Every day, conjugal totalitarianism continues to perpetuate the same misery. This garbage is foisted on the young in the name of spurious, outdated principles, but the unspoken objective is to perpetuate this legacy of suffering and hypocrisy. Ruining lives is still the preferred pastime of venerable old French families, and it is a game about which they know a thing or two. They've had practice. Even today it is still possible to write: 'Families, I hate you'.

I hate you all the more because I didn't rebel until it was too late. Deep down, I was happy being a redneck, a pleb, a noble descendant of a long line of country squires from the Béarn, and I was proud as a peacock to be marrying Anne, my alabaster Aristocat. I was irresponsible, conceited, naive, stupid. But I'm paying for it now. I brought this disaster on myself because, like everyone else, like every one of you reading this now, I thought I was the exception to the rule. Of course I'd be happy. Of course Anne and I would tiptoe between the raindrops. Failure was something that happened to other people. Then one day, love was gone and I woke up with a start. Until that moment, I had forced myself to play the happily married man. But I had been lying to myself for so long that it was inevitable I would one day begin to lie to someone else.

# XII

# Lost Illusions

As children of the sixties, we're far too superficial to deal with marriage. For us, deciding who to marry is like choosing what to watch on TV. If we don't like something, we change the channel. Why do we expect to spend the rest of our lives with someone when we're constantly channel-surfing? In an age when celebrities, politicians, arts, sexes and religions are completely disposable, why do we expect love to be different?

But the most important question is, how did we come to be so obsessed? Why do we try to force ourselves to be happy with one person? Of the 558 documented forms of human society, only twenty-four per cent are monogamous. The majority of animal species are polygamous. As for aliens, Intergalactic Charter X23 banned monogamous relationships on all B#871-type planets aeons ago.

Marriage is beluga caviar with every meal: too much of a good thing and before you know it, you're sick to your stomach. 'Come on, one more little mouthful for mummy. What's the matter? What d'you mean you don't like it? You used to love it!'

Western civilisation must have been terrified of the awe-inspiring power of love to have created an institution guaranteed to put you off love once and for all.

*

According to recent American research, infidelity is biological. The eminent scientist responsible for the study declared infidelity is a *genetic strategy which promotes the survival of the species*. I can see it now: 'Darling, I didn't want to cheat on you, I did it for the survival of the species. No, honestly. Maybe you don't care about these things, but somebody has to worry about the survival of the species! If you think I enjoy going around being unfaithful . . .'

I'm never satisfied: from the moment I find a woman attractive, I fall in love with her; once I'm in love, I want to kiss her; once I've kissed her, I want to sleep with her; once I've slept with her, I want to move in with her; once I've moved in with her, I want to marry her; and as soon as I marry her, I meet someone else. Men are never satisfied, they are always hesitating between temptations. If women really want a relationship to last, all they have to do is never sleep with us and we will happily spend the rest of our lives chasing them.

If you're in love, when exactly did you start to lie? Are you really still excited to be going home to the same person every night? Have you ever said 'I love you' when you didn't really mean it? In every relationship, there comes a critical moment when you yourself have to make the effort. When suddenly 'I love you' doesn't sound the same. For me, it was shaving. Every night I shaved so I wouldn't scratch Anne when I kissed her goodnight. Then, one night, I didn't shave. Anne was already asleep (I'd gone out on my own and come back in at dawn in the pathetic way men do when they're married) so I didn't think it meant anything; after all, she'd never know. In fact it meant I didn't love her any more.

Anybody who's ever thought about getting a divorce has read Dan Franck's *La Séparation*. In the heartbreaking opening scene, a husband realises that his wife doesn't love him any more at the theatre, when he takes her hand and she pulls away. He tries to take her hand again, but she pulls away again. I remember thinking: what a bitch! How could she be so cruel? How hard can it be to let your husband hold your hand?! Until I found myself pulling away when Anne took my hand, or slipped her arm through mine. Sometimes when we were watching TV, she'd rest her hand on my leg. I would look down and the sight of her pale, clammy hand, like a rubber glove, made me wince. It was as if she'd put an octopus on my leg. I felt guilty: I thought, God, what's happening to me? I'm turning into that bitch in the Dan Franck novel. When Anne entwined her fingers with mine, I let her, but I couldn't suppress a frown. I'd get up suddenly and tell her I had to go for a pee, when actually I just had to get away from that hand. Then I'd feel guilty and try to backtrack, and I'd stare at this hand I had once loved. The hand which, before God, I had asked for in marriage. The hand that, three years ago, I would have given my right arm to hold. And suddenly I hated myself, I pitied her, I felt indifferent, I wanted to cry. And I pulled that limp octopus to my heart and kissed it, a wet kiss full of sorrow and sullen anger.

When you look for a way out, it's all over. You know it's all over because it's too late to turn things round, because you don't understand each other, because without even noticing, you've already divorced.

# XIII

# Flirting with Disaster

That night, at some point during my Double-5 Tour, a mate came up to me (I don't remember who or when, much less where) and said:

'Why the long face?'

And I remember saying:

'Because love lasts three years.'

It must have done the trick, because he wandered off. Now, I say it all the time. If someone asks me why I'm looking miserable, I just come out with it:

'Because love lasts three years.'

It sounds cool.

I've even been wondering if maybe it would make a good title for a book.

Love lasts three years. Even if you've been married for forty years, in your heart you know it's true. You remember what you sacrificed, you remember the day you surrendered, the fateful day when you stopped being afraid.

I know that having me tell you that love lasts three years is horrible; it's like watching a magic trick go horribly wrong, like an alarm clock waking you in the middle of a wet dream. But someone has to put an end to this myth of eternal love, the cornerstone of our civilisation, the fount of human misery.

After three years, a couple must divorce, commit suicide or have children: these are the traditional means of proving it's all over.

There are those who claim that, with time, passion is transformed into 'something else', something eternal and beautiful. Something less passionate but less immature. This 'something else', they say, is Love (with a capital L). Let me just say this: fuck that! If this 'something else' really is Love-with-a-capital-L, then I'm happy to leave love to the bored, spineless middle-aged men who want to stay at home with their pipe and slippers. My love may not have a capital L, but at least it soars; it may not last for all eternity, but at least while it does, you can feel it. The 'something else' they call love sounds to me like sour grapes. They've had to settle for second best and now they want to claim that this is as good as love gets. They remind me of those guys who scratch the paintwork of expensive cars because they can't afford one themselves.

An apocalyptic end to a disastrous evening. I feel like ending it all. At about five o'clock in the morning, I phone Adeline H. on her home number – that should give you some idea of the state I was in. She answers: 'Hello? Hello? Who is this?' She sounds rough. I've clearly woken her up. I don't know why she didn't just let her answering machine take it. I don't know what to say. 'Um . . . Sorry if I woke you up . . . I just wanted to say goodnight.' 'WHO IS THIS? ARE YOU OUT OF YOUR MIND? JESUS!' I hang up. I sit with my head in my hands trying to decide whether to take an overdose of Lexomil or hang myself: then again, why not do both? I don't have any rope, but a couple of Paul Smith ties knotted together should do the trick. English designers use durable materials. I stick a Post-it note on the

TV: 'ANY MAN STILL ALIVE AT THE AGE OF 30 IS A MORON.' I'm glad I rented a flat with exposed joists. Now all I have to do is climb up on the chair. That's it. Knock back the tranquillisers with a mouthful of Coke. Now just slip my head into the noose so that when I nod off, I know I won't wake up.

# XIV

# Provisional Resurrection

But I do wake up. I open one eye, then the other. I have two separate headaches, one from the hangover and one from the lump on my forehead that's still visibly swelling. It's past noon, and I feel like a complete idiot lying on the floor beside an upturned chair with a tangle of ties around my neck with a cleaning lady standing over me.

'Carmelita, hi . . . Was, um . . . Was I asleep long?'

'Please you move, I need hoover floor please.'

Then, I see the note on the TV screen: 'ANY MAN STILL ALIVE AT THE AGE OF 30 IS A MORON.' Clearly I must be psychic. Poor me, all I want is for women to love me and I get all depressed because of a little divorce. I should have thought about that before. Now I only have my pain for company. What a complete waste of time – trying to kill myself when I'm already dead.

Suicidal people are completely insufferable. I wanted to leave and now I resent my wife for letting me go. I resent her for showing me what a bastard I am. I resent her for allowing me to start all over again. I resent her for making me face up to my responsibilities. I resent her for forcing me to write this paragraph. I used to hate my life because I felt trapped, now I hate my life because I'm free. So this is what it means to be an adult: you build a sandcastle so you can knock it down, then you build another and another, even though you know that the tide will wash them away?

My eyelids are heavy as nightfall. I've got old this year. How do you know you're getting old? You know you're getting old when it takes three days to recover from a hangover. You know you're getting old when you can't even manage to commit suicide. You know you're getting old when the minute you meet some young people, you turn into a wet blanket. Their youthful eagerness gets on your nerves, their youthful illusions make you feel queasy. You know you're getting old because last night when some girl told you she was born in 1976, you said:

'Oh, I remember '76. That was the year we had the heat wave.'

Since I have no nails left to bite, I go out for something to eat.

# XV

# The Wailing Wall

Even though I know there's no such thing as love, I'm sure that in a year or two's time I'll be proud that once upon a time, I believed in love. They can't take that away from us, Anne: we truly believed. Heads down, we ran straight into a reinforced concrete *muleta*. Don't laugh. You don't see people making fun of Don Quixote, and he tilted at windmills.

For most of my life I have had only one aim: to self-destruct, but once, just once, there was a moment when I wanted to be happy. It's pathetic, I'm ashamed to admit it, but once I felt the tawdry desire to be happy. And this, as I have learned, is by far the surest path to self-destruction. So subconsciously, at least, I'm consistent.

I don't know why I agreed to go round to Jean-Georges' place for dinner. I'm not hungry. I've always made it a point only to eat when I'm hungry. This is what style means: to eat when one is hungry, drink when one is thirsty, fuck when one is horny. But I can't sit around ignoring my friends until I'm starving to death. Jean-Georges has probably invited that glorious gang of freaks I call my dearest friends. We never talk about our problems, we just change the subject to keep despair at bay.

It turns out that I was wrong, because when I get to Jean-Georges', he's on his own. Jean-Georges has decided to listen to my problems, to be there for me. He grabs me by the scruff of the neck and shakes me like a parking meter that swallows ten francs and then refuses to spit out the pay-and-display ticket.

'Last night, when I asked you what the long face was about, you gave me some shit about love lasts three years. Do you think I'm stupid? Do you think you're living in one of your novels? So I suppose this has nothing to do with your divorce coming through? Why don't you just cut the bullshit and tell me what's on your mind? If you can't even do that, then why are we friends?'

I look away so that he doesn't see my eyes are clouded with tears. I fake a cold and have a good sniffle. I mumble:

'What? I don't know what you're on about . . .'

'Don't bullshit me. Who is she? Do I know her?'

And then, my heart heavy, my foot in my mouth, I whisper:

'Her name is Alice.'

# XVI

# Would You Like to Be My Harem?

So, here's the thing: three years ago, Marc and Alice got married. Unfortunately, they didn't marry each other. Marc married Anne and Alice married Antoine. Life is complicated – unless perhaps people seek out complicated situations?

Alice was the other woman. The photo Anne found in Rio was a stunning Polaroid of Alice wearing a bikini on a beach near Rome. In Fregene, to be precise.

Alice and I had been having 'a bit on the side': this is what we call a passionate love affair these days. All over the world, people are pining for their 'bit on the side'. It might be a woman you pass in the street without a second glance. You wouldn't think it to look at her, she keeps her passion hidden, but sometimes you'll catch her crying over some mediocre soap opera, or smiling for no reason in the metro and you'll know what I mean. Often, the relationship is unequal: when a single woman falls in love with a married man who won't leave his wife, it's miserable, contemptible, banal. But Alice and I were already married when we met. It was a relationship of equals. But I was the first to crack: I got divorced, something Alice has no intention of doing. Why would she leave her husband for some lunatic who goes round telling anyone who will listen that love lasts three years?

I could tell Alice that I don't really believe it, but that would be a lie. And I'm sick of lying, sick of sneaking around. Polygamy is perfectly legal in France as long as you lie through your teeth. Having several wives just takes a little imagination and a lot of organisation. I know guys who have a veritable harem, they phone a different woman every night, and the sad thing is that the 'chosen one' comes running. All it takes is a little diplomacy and a little hypocrisy, which I suppose amounts to the same thing. But I'm sick of leading a double life. Being schizophrenic at work is bad enough; I haven't got the energy to be schizophrenic in my spare time too. For once, it would be nice to do just one thing at a time.

Result: I'm on my own again.

Love is a glorious catastrophe: you know you're heading for a brick wall, and still you floor the accelerator; you rush in where angels fear to tread with a smile on your face, always wondering when things will finally fuck up. Love is a failure signposted in advance, an avoidable accident, and still we go back for more. This is what I tell Alice, just before I go down on one knee and propose that we run away together. She turns me down.

# XVII

# The Horns of a Dilemma

One day, catastrophe came into my life and, fuckwit that I am, I haven't managed to get it to move out.

Nothing in the world is more exquisite than unrequited love. This is something I have learned from bitter experience. Nothing could be more painful than loving someone who doesn't love you, and yet it is the most wonderful thing that ever happened to me. Loving someone who loves you is nothing more than narcissism. Unrequited love, now that's true love. All my life, I prayed for some test, some trial, some ordeal which would transform me and unfortunately, my prayers were answered. I am in love with a woman who doesn't love me and not in love with a woman who does. Women are just a means for me to perfect my self-loathing.

> Fan Ch'ih asked: 'What is love?'
> The Master said: 'To rank the effort above the reward may be called love.' (Confucius)

That's all very well, Confucius, but you can hardly expect me to turn my back on the reward either. Now, I'm alone. As soon as Alice found out that Anne had walked out on me, she got cold feet. No phone calls, no messages, no hotel room numbers on my answering machine. I feel like some lovelorn bunny-boiler desperately waiting for her married man to come back. I who have always lived out my life on broad leafy avenues, suddenly find myself haunting the backstreets. A single question runs through my mind, a question that seems to sum up my very existence:

Which is worse: to make love without loving, or to love without making love?

I feel like Tintin's dog, Snowy, when he's on the horns of a dilemma, a tiny angel perched on one shoulder telling him to be good and a devil on the other telling him to be bad. The little angel is telling me to go home to my wife while the devil is telling me go off and fuck Alice. It's a non-stop Jerry Springer show broadcasting live in my head. Why can't the devil just tell me to go back and fuck my wife?

# XVIII

# Highs and Lows

Life is like a sitcom: the same characters playing out the same situations on the same sets and still we're on the edge of our seats. When Alice turned up in my life it was a shock, it was like someone from the cast of *Sex and the City* showing up on the set of *Seinfeld*.

Alice is an ostrich, that is the only way to describe her. She is tall and wild, and at the first sign of danger she sticks her head in the sand. Her slender, never-ending legs (two in number) support a sensual body bearing ripe fruits (of the same number). Long, straight, coal-black hair frames a face that is passionate yet gentle. Alice has a body designed to strike terror into the loins of the most happily married man. A man who never dreamed of being unfaithful, who never dreamed he'd have it so good. This is the difference between Alice and an ostrich (that and the fact that she doesn't lay 2lb eggs; something I would later have the opportunity to verify).

I remember the first time I saw Alice. It was at my grandmother's funeral. I was there on my own, since my wife, understandably, found such family gatherings tedious. Having to deal with one's own family is bad enough without having to deal with someone else's . . . In fact, I had told her not to come; after all, wherever Bonne Maman was now, she was hardly likely to comment on Anne's absence. Maybe I had a premonition that something was going to happen.

Everyone in the church was staring at my grandfather, waiting for him to shed a tear. I sat silently praying: 'PLEASE GOD, DON'T LET HIM CRY.' But I had not reckoned on the priest's secret weapon: the memories of fifty years of happy marriage Bon Papa had spent with Bonne Maman. My grandfather's eyes – and the man is a retired colonel – began to well with tears. When the first tear spilled over, it opened the floodgates and the whole family began to sob, staring in stunned silence at the coffin. It seemed impossible that Bonne Maman was in that wooden box, impossible that she had had to die before I realised how much I loved her. Jesus Christ, when I wasn't walking out on those I loved, they were dying. I started to cry hysterically. I'm easily led.

When at last I looked up through the blur, I saw a beautiful dark-haired woman staring at me. Alice had seen me snot-nosed with grief. I don't know whether it was the emotion, or the incongruity of the situation, but I felt instantly attracted to this mysterious creature in the tight black sweater. Later, Alice told me that her first impression when she saw me was how handsome I was: we'll chalk up that lapse to an overactive maternal instinct. All that mattered at that moment was that the attraction was mutual – she wanted to comfort me, I could tell. This incident taught me a valuable lesson: the best thing to do at a funeral is fall in love.

Alice, I discovered, was one of my cousin's friends. She introduced me to her husband Antoine, a nice guy – too nice, probably. As she kissed my tear-streaked cheeks she realised that I realised that she'd noticed that I'd noticed that she'd looked at

me the way she looked at me. I'll never forget the first words
I said to her:

'You've got great bone structure.'

I had time to study her. A young woman, twenty-seven years
old, simply beautiful. The tremor of her eyelashes. A sulky laugh
to make the hardest heart leap in a chest that suddenly feels
constricted. Everything about her was magnificent: her shy
glance, her windswept hair, the curve of the small of her back,
her dazzling teeth. She was Claudia Cardinale in *The Leopard*.
She was Bettie Page stretched out to 5'10". She was tenderly
wild, serenely flirtatious, shamelessly reticent. A friend, an
enemy.

How was it possible that I'd never met her? What was the point
in knowing hundreds of people when she wasn't one of them?

The churchyard was cold. You know what I'm getting at: yes,
her nipples were hard under her tight black sweater. Her breasts
were pert. Her face had an innocence belied by her sensual
body. I've always been a sucker for the face of an angel on the
body of a whore. It's my favourite oxymoron. I've got a thing
for dichotomy.

At that moment I knew I would do anything to get into her
life, her heart, her bed and whatever else was on offer. This
woman was not an ostrich, she was an acrobat: she could turn
men head over heels.

'Do you know the Basque country?'

'No, but I've heard it's pretty.'

'Not pretty, glorious. It's a pity that we're both married, otherwise we could have run away and raised a family on a farm in
the Basque country.'

'Would we have sheep?'

'Of course we'd have sheep. And ducks for the foie gras, and cows for the milk and chickens for the eggs and a cock for the chickens, and a short-sighted elephant, a dozen giraffes and a flock of ostriches just like you.'

'I'm not an ostrich, I'm an acrobat.'

'Hey – not fair – no mind-reading!'

After she left, I wandered, happy and heedless, through the streets of Guéthary, the village where Paul-Jean Toulet was born, and where I'd spent my idyllic childhood. Whereas usually I detest walking, now I sauntered, carefree and animated (nobody seemed to notice: people always do strange things after a funeral), I wandered along the sea front, alive to every rock, every wave, every grain of sand. My heart was brimming over. The very sky seemed to belong to me. The Basque country brought me more luck than the beaches of Rio. I smiled up at the listless clouds scudding across the heavens and at Bonne Maman looking down on me and smiling.

# XIX

# Flee Happiness Lest It Run Away

In life, you either live with someone or you can desire them. To desire something you already have goes against nature. This is why even a perfect marriage can be torn apart by any passing stranger. You might be married to the most beautiful woman in the world, but one day a woman will walk into your life and hit you like an overdose of Viagra. And Alice was not just any woman, she was a woman in a tight black sweater. Tight black sweaters have been known to change the course of two lives.

My problem is I have a childlike fascination with anything new, a morbid desire to yield to each of the myriad temptations the future has to offer. I'm amazed by how much more aroused I am by the new than by the familiar, but it's hardly unusual. Most people would prefer to read a book they haven't read, see a play they've never seen, vote for anyone rather than the arsehole who's already President.

My most cherished memories of Anne all date from before our marriage. Marriage murders mystery. You fall in love with some mysterious creature, you marry her and suddenly the mysterious creature has disappeared to be replaced by your wife. YOUR WIFE! It's a terrible anticlimax! Men should spend their whole lives chasing after unattainable women. (In this, as it turned out, Alice was ideal.)

Love is fundamentally flawed: in order to be happy, people need stability, but love is alluring precisely because it is tentative. Happiness is based on certainty; love thrives on doubt and ambiguity. Marriage is designed not to keep love alive, but to make people happy. And falling in love is not the best way to find happiness – if it were, we'd know by now. I'm not sure if I'm making myself clear, but I know what I mean: what I'm trying to say is that marriage is a mixture of things that don't sit easily together.

Back in Paris, everything was suddenly different. Anne was no longer on a pedestal. We made love half-heartedly. My life was falling apart. You know the ninth circle of hell? Well, I'd just moved into the flat below.

There is no happy love.

There is no happy love.

THERE IS NO HAPPY LOVE.

How many times do I have to say it before you get it through your thick skull, arsehole?

# XX

# Things Fall Apart

When a woman looks at you the way Alice looked at me, there are only two possibilities: either she's a prick-tease, in which case you're in trouble; or she's not a prick-tease, in which case you're really in trouble.

There I was, happy as a clam in my little hermetically sealed shell and suddenly Alice comes along, picks me up, prises my mouth wide open and squeezes lemon juice all over me.

'Almighty God,' I prayed, 'please make this woman love her husband because if she doesn't, I'm in deep shit!'

I didn't contact Alice. I thought my feelings would fade away, and in time, they did – but not quite as I had hoped. Instead, much to my annoyance, it was my feelings for Anne which faded. There is too much heartbreak in this world, but nothing can compare to the heartbreak of a woman who feels the love she had slowly die. Love does not disappear overnight, it trickles away inexorably like sand through an hourglass. To bloom, a woman needs a man's love, just as a flower needs sunshine, at least that's how I see it. Without me to gaze at her, Anne began to wilt and I couldn't do anything about it. Marriage, time, Alice, the movement of the planets, tight black sweaters, the

Maastricht treaty, everything seemed to be conspiring against our love.

I was abandoning my wife, but I was saying goodbye to a part of myself. The most difficult thing was not giving up on Anne, it was giving up on the love story we had shared. I felt like a man abandoning a long-cherished project: disappointed and relieved.

# XXI

# Question Marks

Nowadays, when I run into a friend in the street, it goes like this:

'Hey, what's up? How's life?'

'Shit, you?'

'Shit.'

'Right . . . Well . . . See you.'

'See you.'

Or a friend will tell me a joke.

'What's the difference between love and herpes?'

' . . . '

'Go on, have a guess!'

' . . . '

'For God's sake, it's easy: herpes is forever.'

' . . . '

I don't laugh, I don't see what's funny about that. Maybe I lost my sense of humour.

It is a lesson in humility when you discover that the questions that haunt you are the same questions that haunt everybody.

Am I doing the right thing?

Am I a bastard?

What is the meaning of death?

Am I going to make the same mistakes my parents made?

Does happiness exist?

Is it possible to fall in love without it all ending in blood, sweat, tears and spunk?

Surely it must be possible for me to earn A LOT MORE money for A LOT LESS effort?

Which sunglasses should I wear on the beach in Formentera?

After several weeks agonisingly wrestling with my conscience, I come to the following decision: if your wife is turning into a girlfriend, it's time to ask your girlfriend to become your wife.

# XXII

# Reunion

I met Alice for the second time at some birthday party hardly worth mentioning. Suffice it to say that one of Anne's friends had just got a year older, an event somebody thought worthy of celebrating. When I spotted Alice's lithe figure (her delicate, supple skin), I was pouring a glass of champagne for Anne and went on filling to a point somewhere above the rim, soaking the tablecloth. Alice and her husband were drinking. My face flushed. I knocked back my whisky. I had to concentrate on my feet so as not to stumble, making it possible to hide my blushes behind my mane of hair. I deserted my wife and rushed off to the loo to check my hair, make sure I'd shaved, take off my glasses, dust the dandruff off my shoulders, pluck the stray hair peeking from my left nostril. I tried to decide what to do. Should I ignore Alice? After all, when you really fancy someone, you're supposed to behave as if they don't exist. But if I ignore her, she might leave and the idea of never seeing her again was torture. I had to find a way to talk to her without talking to her. I wandered back to the party and walked right past Alice, pretending not to see her.

'Marc! Are you not even going to say hello?'

'Oh, Alice! What a surprise! Sorry, I didn't recognise you! I'm . . . really . . . happy . . . to . . . see . . . you . . . again . . .'

'Me too! How are things?'

She was studiously polite, uninterested, nightmarish, constantly looking over my shoulder.

'You remember Antoine?'

We exchanged a glacial handshake.

'Aren't you going to introduce us to your wife?'

'I think she's in the kitchen putting candles on the birthday cake.'

As I said this, the lights went out, and the drone of 'Happy Birthday' began. In all the confusion, Alice disappeared. I watched as she took Antoine's hand and they took off as the Birthday Girl was laughing about her age to thunderous cheers from her equally ancient friends.

I am sure most of you will have seen a building implosion on television. You know the kind of thing, when they bring down a twenty-storey skyscraper with strategically placed explosives. There is the short countdown and then you see the building shudder and collapse into itself in a cloud of dust and a hail of gravel. That's how I felt at that moment as I watched Alice and Antoine heading for the door. I had to do something. I can still see it in slow motion, as if it happened yesterday. I followed them and while Antoine was rummaging through the coats, Alice turned her dark, brimming eyes on me and I whispered:

'I don't believe it, Alice, it can't be you . . . What about everything we said last month in Guéthary? What about our ostrich farm?'

Her face softened. She looked down and, in a whisper so soft I thought I might have dreamed it, she said two words as she surreptitiously stroked my hand before disappearing with her husband:

'I'm scared . . .'

\*

From that moment, my fate was sealed. Even as Anne was indignantly asking 'Who the hell was that?', my skyscraper was swiftly rising from the dust cloud. The demolition video rewound all the way back to the day the building was opened: 14 July, a brass band plays, there are fireworks and Chinese lanterns, the mayor of Parly 2 gives a speech. The whole thing is being broadcast live on France 3! The crowd is suicidally happy. Bang! Bang! They gleefully top themselves! It's mass suicide! It's a Jonestown holiday! A Temple Solaire rally. People burst out laughing as they die. It's madness, absolute fucking madness!

The best parties are those that happen only in our imagination.

# XXIII

# Leave

I'm fascinated by the intense, palpable, tremulous, electric tension that can build up between a man and a woman who barely know each other simply because they're attracted to each other and are trying their best to hide the fact.

They don't need to say a word. They can say it all with a glance, with a look. Uncouth people refer to it as erotic, when in fact it is pornographic – by which I mean it is honest. The world could crumble, but you have eyes only for her eyes. Suddenly, in your heart of hearts, you know that all it would take is a word and you would leave everything for this woman with whom you have exchanged barely three words. 'Leave' is the most beautiful word in the world. You are ready to use it. 'Let's leave.' 'We have to leave.' 'One day, we will take trains leaving' (Blondin). Your bags are packed, the past is no more than a jumble you must try to forget, for today you are reborn. You know you are hurtling towards an irrevocable decision, but you don't slow down. You know this is the only way out. You know you are about to hurt someone you love. You know you should spare them this pain, you should reason with them, take your time, think things through, but the word 'Leave!' is impossible to resist. To start over. To go back to square one. It is as if you have spent your whole life underwater, a child holding his breath. Now, the future is the bare shoulder of a strange girl. Life has offered you a way out; destiny is offering you a second chance.

Love at first sight may seem superficial, but there is nothing more profound; for this a man will do anything; accept every flaw; forgive every imperfection; in fact he will seek out flaws to forgive, for we are always attracted by another person's weaknesses.

Alice was distressed. She was scared of me! I was petrified. But never in my life had I been more happy to frighten someone.

I couldn't know that I would regret it.

# XXIV

# The Beauty of Beginnings

During one of our secret meetings, after we'd made love three times, whimpering with pleasure in the Hôtel Henri-IV (place Dauphine), I took Alice to the Café Beaubourg. I'm not sure why, given that I hate 'designer' cafés. Designer cafés exist for tourists and rednecks so that Parisians can have lunch in the Café de Flore in peace. Afterwards, as we stepped out onto the esplanade of the Pompidou Centre, we stopped in front of the Génitron, the digital clock counting off the seconds until the year 2000.

'Look, Alice. That clock symbolises our love.'

'What do you mean?'

'I mean the countdown has started . . . The time will come when you'll find me boring, irritating, when you'll yell at me for leaving the toilet seat up, when I slump in front of the TV instead of coming to bed, when you'll cheat on me the way you're cheating on Antoine right now.'

'Why do you always do this . . . Why can't you just be happy that we're together instead of worrying about the future?'

'Because we have no future. Look at the seconds ticking away, each one bringing us closer to unhappiness . . . We've got three years . . . Right now, everything is wonderful, but by my calculations, it'll all be over by . . . 15 March 1997.'

'Why don't I just finish with you now and save time?'

'No, wait . . . I'm sorry. Forget I said anything.'

I suddenly realised I should have kept my mouth shut instead of spouting my half-arsed theories.

'Why don't you break up with Antoine instead?' I asked. 'We could go and live in the Little House on the Prairie and watch our kids play in The Secret Garden . . .'

'That's right, make a joke about it! Marc, you're a lovely guy, I don't understand why you always have to spoil what little time we have together with these fits of jealousy.'

'Darling, if you ever cheat on me, I promise you two things: first, I'll kill myself, then I'll come round and make a scene you'll never forget.'

We walked on, an illicit couple, strolling side by side, gazing into each other's eyes, though we could never hold hands in case we ran into friends of her husband or my wife.

With Alice, I discovered how to be gentle. She taught me how to be honest. I think that's what I most loved about Alice. The first time you fall in love, you're looking for perfection, the second time, you're looking for honesty.

The sexiest thing about a woman is her health. I love a woman who radiates health! I want to watch her frolic, and laugh, to stuff herself silly! Her teeth should be white as the whites of her eyes, her mouth as fresh as a newly-made bed, her lips like cherries whose every kiss is a jewel, her skin as taut as a tom-tom, her breasts as round as a pair of boules, her clavicle delicate as a wishbone, her legs golden as Tuscany, and her arse as round as a baby's cheek. But most importantly she should never wear make-up. She shouldn't smell of perfume and cigarettes but of milk and sweat.

The litmus test is the swimming pool because here, a woman

reveals her true self: a brainy woman will read in the shade of her broad-brimmed hat, a sporty woman organises a game of water polo, a vain woman will work on her tan, while a hypochondriac is smearing herself with SPF 50 . . . If you meet a woman who hovers on the edge of a swimming pool afraid to get her hair wet, run. If she giggles and dives right in, you should dive in after her.

Believe me: I did everything in my power not to fall in love – once bitten, twice disfigured – but I couldn't stop thinking about Alice. There were times when I despised her, when I thought she was a pathetic spineless bitch, pretending to be in love when all she really cared about was trying to save her pitiful marriage, a miserable selfish coward, with the high-pitched voice and fashion sense of Olive Oyl. Then, a minute later, I'd see a picture of her, or hear her sweet voice on the phone, or she would suddenly appear before me and I would fall at her feet, dazzled by the sheer force of her delicate beauty, her breathtaking eyes, her velvety skin, her long, flyaway silky hair, and suddenly she was a wild indomitable savage, a fiery squaw, she was Esmeralda and my God, at that moment I thanked heaven that I had met such a creature.

Here is a simple test to discover whether or not you are in love: if you begin to miss your lover only a few hours after seeing her, you're not in love; if you were, ten minutes would have been enough to make your life a living hell.

# XXV

# Thank You, Wolfgang

Cheating on your wife is nothing to worry about as long as she never finds out. I think lots of men cheat on their wives for the sense of danger they used to feel when they first went out with their wives. From that point of view, you could say that adultery is an affirmation of marriage. Then again, maybe not. At least I think I'd have had a hard time convincing Anne.

I remember the last time Anne and I had dinner together. I wish I didn't, but I do. Bad times, they say, make for good memories. Every word, every detail is etched on my memory, filed away under 'bad times'. If reincarnation exists, I want to come back as a video recorder so I can erase these painful memories.

At first, Anne blamed me for everything, then she blamed herself for blaming me, which only made me feel worse. I told her it was all my fault, that I had been starring in my own private movie: why else would I have cut my hair so short during the three years we were married? My hair was long before we got married, now at last I was letting it grow back. Like Samson, without my hair I was weak. What was worse was the fact that I hadn't observed the social niceties, I had never asked her father for his daughter's hand in marriage, thereby meaning our union was null and void. She laughed at my jokes. I felt like a shit, but she just smiled sadly as if she'd always known we would end up here, in this pretty restaurant, staring across the white tablecloth glowing in the candlelight, chatting like old friends. In the end, we didn't even cry. Strangely, it's possible to leave your wife, break every vow you ever made to her, and still sit across the table from her and not make a meal of things.

That was when she told me she'd met someone else, someone older, gentler and more famous than me. It had been going on for a while (the husband is always the last to know), she'd met him through work. This was something I honestly hadn't expected. I went ballistic:

'Young women going out with old blokes are as bad as old blokes copping off with young girls. It's too easy!'

'I'd rather go out with a good-looking, confident older guy than an ugly neurotic younger one any day.'

I don't know why I thought Anne would spend her life a tearful, heartbroken widow. I don't know why the fact that she was seeing someone bothered me. Well, actually, I do know. My pride was hurt. Pompous git that I am, I thought she couldn't live without me, when in fact she would soon be living with someone else. What did I expect? Did I think she would kill herself? That she'd pine away? There I was dreaming of Alice, imagining I was some kind of playboy surrounded by women and all the while Anne was dreaming of my replacement and happily cheating on me and making sure that everyone knew about it. I deserved it. It was poetic justice. On my way home in the car, I listed to Mozart on the radio.

All beauty is destined to ugliness, youth will always wither, life is nothing more than a long, slow decline, we die a little every day. Luckily, we still have Mozart. I wonder how many lives Mozart has saved?

228

# XXVI

# Hot Sex Chapter

It's time we got down to the nitty-gritty – you know what I'm talking about: sex. Most of the stuck-up tarts I grew up with seemed to think sex involved lying on your back while some drunken moron in a smoking-jacket jiggles around on top, shoots his load and rolls off, snoring. Their sex education was conducted in a series of society parties, private members' clubs and Saint-Tropez nightspots by the worst fucks on God's earth: Posh Boys. The sexual failings of the Posh Boy stem from the fact that, from his earliest childhood, he's been accustomed to getting whatever he wants without having to work for it. It's not that he's selfish (in bed, ALL men are selfish), it's just that nobody's ever told him there's a difference between a girl and a Porsche (if you prang a girl, Daddy doesn't stop your pocket money).

Anne, thankfully, didn't fall into this category, but she wasn't particularly interested in sex. The wildest sex we ever had was on our honeymoon in Goa after smoking jimson weed. Spurting, pumping, panting, spunking. We needed to smoke just to relax in the clammy monsoon air. But unfortunately this sexual high point was just a hallucinogenic one-off. In fact, on our honeymoon, I was so in love with Anne that I even let her beat me at table tennis, proof, if proof were needed, that I wasn't in my right mind. So now you know, Anne, when we were on our honeymoon I deliberately threw that table tennis game, okay??

Sexual compatibility is a lottery: two people can both enjoy sex and still be incompatible. You think it will come in time, but these things never change. Sexuality is skin-deep, and like everything skin-deep (racism, acne . . .) it is deeply unfair.

To make matters worse, our affection just got in the way. It's disturbing to find your sex life suddenly switches from hard-core to baby-talk. The minute you find you're no longer moaning 'Oh yeah, gonna fuck your face, you little slut' and have started burbling 'izza luvvy bunny gonna gimme tickle-wickle with his 'ickle wee-wee', it's time to pull the emergency cord. It happens quickly: people's voices start to change after a few short months living together. A big hairy stud with a booming voice will start cooing like a baby. The smoky Gauloise voice of a sexy vamp will start to sound like a little girl cooing over a kitten. Our sex life was ruined by inflection.

And then there is probably the most powerful turn-off in the world: Conjugal Duty. If you go for a couple of days without having sex, it's nothing serious, you don't talk about it. But after four or five days, the spectral fear of Conjugal Duty raises its head. A week later, both of you are wondering if there's some-thing wrong and what should be pleasurable expectation starts to feel like a burden. Go for another week without having sex and you'll be so stressed, you'll have to masturbate in the bath-room staring at porn mags just to get it up: by this stage, only one thing is certain – when you finally have sex it will be a disaster, the very antithesis of passion. That's Conjugal Duty.

Our generation are woefully misinformed about the subject of sex. We think we know it all because we have satellite porn channels and our parents were part of the so-called sexual revolution. But everyone knows there was no sexual revolution. As far as sex and marriage are concerned, nothing has changed for a century. Sex in the late twentieth century is exactly the same as it was in the late nineteenth century – and considerably less enlightened than it was at the end of the eighteenth. Men are macho, awkward and shy, while women are uptight, uncomfortable with their bodies and hung up on the idea that people will think they're nymphos. Just look at the huge viewing figures for television programmes about sex and the tiny percentage of teenagers who use condoms and you'll realise we're completely incapable of having a normal conversation on the subject. And if kids in general are sexually inept, nice middle-class kids haven't got a clue.

Alice was never like that. She thinks of sex not as a duty, but as a game where it's worth learning the rules in advance if only so you can break them. Alice has no hang-ups, she collects fantasies, she wants to try everything. When we were together, I made up for thirty years of lost time. Alice taught me how to caress. Women like to be stroked lightly with the tips of the fingers, teased with the tip of the tongue; how was I supposed to know unless someone told me? I discovered you could make love almost anywhere (car parks, lifts, in the toilets in night-clubs, trains and aeroplanes, and not just in the toilets – I discovered you could have sex in fields, in the water, in the sunshine) and you could have different kinds of sex (S&M, M&S) in all sorts of positions (The Butterfly, Doggie-Style, The Perfumed Garden, The Torture Garden, The Ball Juice Dispenser, The Petrol Pump, The Snake Swallower, Demonic Dominatrix, or a free gang-bang at Les Chadelles). For her, I went beyond heterosexual, homosexual, bisexual; I became omnisexual. Why limit yourself?

231

I'd be happy for us to have sex with animals, insects, flowers, seaweed, knick-knacks, furniture, stars, anything that will have us. I also discovered myself inventing shocking stories, each wilder than the last, just so I could whisper them into her ear while we were making love. Some day, I'll publish an anthology that will shock the people who think they know me. I became a bona fide polymorphous pervert, or, as we say in French, a *bon vivant*. I don't see why you should wait to be an old age pensioner to be a dirty old man.

All in all I learned that if a torrid sexual affair can sometimes become a loving relationship, the reverse is rare indeed.

# XXVII

# Letters (I)

First letter to Alice:

Dear Alice,

You are a wonder. I don't see why people can't tell you you're a wonder, just because your name is Alice.

My head is spinning. They shouldn't allow women like you to go to my grandmother's funeral. Apologies for this short note. It was the only way for me to feel close to you this weekend.

Marc

No reply.

Second letter to Alice:

Alice,

I was just wondering . . . are you the love of my life?

There is something going on between us, isn't there?

You told me you're scared. I don't know what I'm supposed to say. I know you think this is just a game to me, but I've never been more serious in all my life.

I don't know what to do. I want to see you but I know I

shouldn't. Last night I was thinking about you as I performed my conjugal duty. It's reprehensible. You have torn my world apart, but I have no wish to do the same to yours. This will be my last letter, though it will be some time before I forget you.

Marc

P.S. 'When we lie, when we tell a woman that we love her, we might believe that we are lying, but something compelled us to say those words, therefore they are true.' (Raymond Radiguet)

No reply. It was not my last letter.

# XXVIII

# The Depths of Despair

I'm back, the knight of the living dead.

If I had the choice, I would be melancholy, it has a certain elegance; instead I alternate between liquefaction and deliquescence. I am a zombie baying at the moon because I'm still alive. The only cure for a migraine like this is 1,000mg of Aspegic, but I can't take any more because I have a pain in my stomach. If only I'd hit rock bottom, but I'm still tumbling, tumbling, and there's nothing to break my fall.

I wander the city aimlessly. I come to stare up at the building where you and Antoine live. When I first started flirting with you, it was just a game, now here I am, loitering in your doorway, breathless. Warning: love may cause respiratory problems.

There is a light in your apartment. Perhaps you're having dinner, or watching TV, or listening to music and thinking about me, or not thinking about me, or maybe you and Antoine are . . . Oh, please God don't tell me you're doing that. I stand here bleeding in the street, but there is no blood, instead I'm bleeding inside, I'm drowning in air. Passers-by wonder why I come here every day to stare up at this building. Perhaps some magnificent architectural detail they've missed. Or maybe, with my three-day stubble and rat's-nest hair, they assume I'm homeless.

'Look, darling, round here even homeless people wear agnès b.'
'Shut up, you idiot, can't you see he's a dealer?'

May is the cruellest month, breeding long weekends out of
the dead land: May Day, Armistice Day, Ascension, Pentecost –
long holiday weekends without Alice, stretching out into eternity. It is a penance imposed by the State and the Catholic
Church for breaking their commandments. It is a crash course
in suffering.

Nothing interests me now. Alice occupies my every waking
thought. Everything which once constituted my moronic four-
grand-a-month lifestyle seems meaningless – going to the
movies, eating, writing, reading, sleeping, dancing the Jerk,
working. Without Alice, the world is drained of colour. Suddenly,
it's like I'm sixteen again. I even bought her favourite perfume
so I could inhale her scent and dream of her, but her perfume
cannot capture the entrancing dusky drowsy skin long loving
legs stunning slender shapeliness languid siren hair. That's something you can't bottle.

In the twentieth century, love is a telephone that never rings,
it is afternoons spent listening to footsteps on the stairs, footsteps like so many false hopes, since you left a message on the
answering machine at noon cancelling our assignation. Just
another tawdry tale of adultery, I'm sorry. I know it's not terribly
original. But it is the worst thing that has ever happened to me.
This is a book written by a spoiled child, dedicated to all those
fools too righteous to be happy. A book about the bad guys,
the people who deserve no pity. A book for those who are not
supposed to feel lonely since they walked away from their
marriage, but who feel lonely just the same, a loneliness all the
more unbearable since they know that they have brought it on
themselves. Because love is not simply a matter of hurting or
being hurt. Sometimes it can be both.

# XXIX

# The South Bitch Diet

These days, being alone has become a shameful illness. We are desperate not to be alone, because being alone forces us to think. If Descartes were alive, his axiom would not be 'I think, therefore I am', but 'I am alone, therefore I think'. No one wants to be lonely, since loneliness gives us time to think. The more we think, the more intelligent we are, ergo more depressed.

I don't believe anything exists. I don't believe in anything. I don't even see the point of myself. My life is of no use to me. What's on cable tonight?

There is one piece of good news: depression is great for losing weight. People don't talk much about The Depressive Diet, but it's very effective. Put on a few extra pounds? Get a divorce, fall in love with someone who doesn't love you, spend your days alone, brooding on your pain and watch those excess pounds melt away. Before you know it, you'll be slim and beautiful – something you can use to your advantage, assuming you survive your depression.

It's such a pity that I'm in love. Otherwise I could make the most of being single. When I was in college, I loved being single. Every woman seemed beautiful to me. 'There are no ugly women,' I used to say, 'only small vodka glasses.' This was not merely the ramblings of an apprentice alcoholic, I truly believed it was true. 'Every woman has something: it might be her smile, or the way she sighs, the way she twists her ankle or a wayward lock of hair. Even a complete troll can have hidden depths. Maybe even Mimie Mathy has hidden talents.' And then I'd give that rumbling laugh, the laugh I used to use to punctuate my jokes before I knew the meaning of loneliness.

Nowadays, when I get drunk, I just mumble to myself like a tramp. I head for 88 rue Saint-Denis where I wank in a video booth flicking between 124 channels of porn. Some guy sucking a black guy's cock. Zap. A girl in bondage gear having wax dripped on her tongue while electrodes are attached to her shaven pussy. Zap. A peroxide blonde with silicone tits swallowing a mouthful of cum. Zap. A guy in a mask piercing a Dutch girl's nipple as she howls 'Yes, Master'. Zap. A girl with a butt-plug up her arse and a dildo in her vagina. Zap. Cum shot over two lesbians with clothes-pegs attached to nipple and clitoris. Zap. Fat pregnant woman. Zap. Double fist-fuck. Zap. Some guy pissing in a Thai girl's mouth. Zap. Shit, I've run out of change, I haven't come yet and now I'm too drunk to get it up. I talk too loudly in the sex shop, wave my arms around, buy a bottle of poppers. I try to befriend the alcoholics staggering along the rue Saint-Denis yelling about how once upon a time they could have had any girl they wanted. But they won't let me join their gang. In fact, they beat me up and teach me what it really means to suffer. I crawl home, stinking of poppers, drunker than I've been in years. I feel a terrible urge to throw up and I need to take a shit, but I can't do both at the same time. I decide to deal with the diarrhoea first, I sit on the bog and a foul molten lava hits the porcelain, then suddenly the urge to vomit is too much. I turn round and gag on bilious acid as it tears at my throat. I am squatting on the floor of the toilet in a cloud of disinfectant, my arse hanging out, when suddenly I get the shits again and I end up spraying a litre of pestilential liquid shit over the toilet door, sobbing and bawling for Mummy.

# XXX

# Letters (II)

It was the third letter that did the trick. I'd like to thank the Post Office: phones, faxes and email will never compare to a love letter and the dangerous beauty of dangerous liaisons.

Dear Alice,

    I will wait for you every night at seven o'clock on the bench at the place Dauphine. Come, don't come, but I shall be there waiting, every night, starting tonight.

    Marc

I waited for you in the rain on Monday. I waited for you in the rain on Tuesday. Wednesday, it didn't rain, and you came (sounds like a love song by Yves Duteil).

'You came.'

'It looks that way.'

'Why didn't you come on Monday or Tuesday?'

'It was raining . . .'

'Why I oughta . . . buy you an umbrella.'

You smiled. Fantômette veiled by a mane of hair, a portent of recondite pleasures to come. A fresh-faced girl sprung from a Manga comic who smiles without weighing the pros and cons. I held your hand as if it were a delicate artefact. I tried to break the awkward silence. Something . . .

'Alice, I think . . .'

You said:

'Shhh.'

And you leaned down and kissed me. Or maybe I was dreaming – surely something so wonderful could not be happening to me?

I tried again:

'Alice, you can still walk away. But you have to do it now, because if you don't, I'll fall in love with you and you don't know me but I can be a real pain when I'm in love . . .'

This time, you silenced me with your tongue, and at that moment the massed violins from every movie ever made were like fingernails on a blackboard compared to the music in my head.

And if you think that makes me a fool, well fuck you.

# XXXI

# L'Amant

I rarely go to the place Dauphine these days, unless, like tonight, I'm drunk enough to face it. I come and sit on the bench where we first kissed. The passing boats bathe the Pont-Neuf in light. A few yards further along, we could have been les amants du Pont-Neuf. I'm cold, I'm waiting for you. It's been six months since our first kiss, and still I wait. I would never have believed I could have come to this. I'm being punished, forced to atone for some sin, why else would someone put me through this? I wake up in tears and I cry myself to sleep and in between I spend my day wallowing in self-pity. I dreamed of being Laclos and I've wound up being Musset. Love is beyond all understanding. It is impossible to understand the love two people share, and more impossible still to understand love when it happens to you. When I was twenty, I could still keep my emotions under control, now I don't even know my own mind. The most upsetting thing is seeing how much my love of Alice has taken the place of what I once felt for Anne, as if these love affairs were connected vessels. I'm horrified to realise how rash I was. This ridiculous charade, the dilemma of choosing between my wife and my lover might never have happened, just one person replacing another, quietly, with no big fuss, as if tiptoeing into my mind. Surely it must be possible to love someone without taking that love from someone else? Because that is my crime ... Here I am sitting in the place Dauphine and it is my ex-wife I am thinking of, I am thinking of you, Anne ...

Maybe some day, Anne, years from now, we'll run into each other in some bright space, the world around and trees and sunlight and – I don't know – birds singing like they did on our wedding day, and in all that commotion we glance at each other and think about the old days, the days when we were twenty, when we shared our first hopes, our first defeats, when we dreamed together, when we kissed the sky before it caved in and buried us. Because the time we shared is ours, Anne, and no one can ever take it from us.

# XXXII

# Dunno

There were many secret rendezvous on the place Dauphine. Many secret dinners at Chez Paul or at Delfino. Countless stolen afternoons at the Hôtel Henri-IV. In the end, the receptionist knew us so well that she spared us the knowing look, the awkward: 'No luggage?' After all, we rented our room – Room 32 – by the month. Every time we left it, it smelled of love-making.

Between orgasms, I couldn't help but interrogate you.

'Jesus Christ, Alice, I love you from the soles of your feet to the split ends of your hair, but where is this thing going?'

'Dunno.'

'Are you going to leave Antoine?'

'Dunno.'

'Maybe we should get a place together?'

'Dunno.'

'Or maybe we should just leave things the way they are?'

'Dunno.'

'But what the fuck are we going to do?'

'Dunno.'

'Why do you always say "Dunno"?'

'Dunno.'

*

I was being too logical. I would hear the word 'Dunno' again and again, I should simply have accepted it.

But sometimes, sometimes, I couldn't stand it any more.

'Leave him! LEAVE HIM!'

'Stop! STOP ASKING ME TO LEAVE HIM!'

'Just do what I did, get a divorce FUCK'S SAKE!'

'No way. I'm scared, I've always been scared that for you, our love is beautiful because it can never be. If I were free, I'm scared you wouldn't love me any more.'

'NOT TRUE, NOT TRUE, ABSOLUTELY NOT TRUE.'

But in my heart of hearts, I was afraid that maybe it was true. Deaf-mutes talked more easily than we did.

# XXXIII

# The Impossible Decrystallisation

I suppose I have to explain how I died. Remember in *Rebel Without a Cause*, James Dean and a bunch of other idiots play 'chicken'? The rules of the game are simple: you all drive your cars towards a cliff and brake at the last possible moment and the guy who brakes last has the biggest balls. Let's just say the size of his cock is directly proportional to the time that elapses before he floors the brake. Invariably in a game of chicken, some fool ends up at the bottom of the cliff in a Chevy the size of a sardine can. Well, the longer Alice and I were together, the more we realised that we were driving towards the edge of a cliff. What I didn't know was that I would be the fuckwit who wouldn't brake until it was too late.

The fundamental rule when having an affair is you never fall in love. Together you share passionate, electrifying, secret trysts in which you get to feel like a hero without taking the risks. But you can never allow your feelings to interfere or in the end you will confuse sex for love, and then you're lost.

It was an easy mistake to make, after all it is so much more pleasurable to make love when you are in love. It makes a woman feel as if the foreplay goes on forever; it makes a man feel that it is over in a trice. Our selfishness was our undoing. Alice and I pretended to be in love simply so that our orgasms would be more intense, until we realised we really were in love. In love, nothing is more effective than the power of suggestion: unfortunately, it only works one way. By the time you realise it's happening, it's too late. We thought we were just playing, but we were playing with fire. We were already floating above the abyss, like those cartoon characters who run over the edge of a cliff, look at the camera, look down, look back at the camera and only then do they finally fall. 'That's all, folks!'

After Anne and I broke up, I remember that every time I went out everyone I met would ask in a slightly stilted tone, 'Where's Anne? What's Anne doing these days? Why didn't Anne come with you? How is Anne anyway?' And I'd say one of the following:

'She's been working.'

'Isn't she here? I was just looking for her. I've got a date with my wife!'

'She decided to give the party a miss. Between you and me, I should have listened to her, she's got a sixth sense when it comes to these things. It's a lousy party. Oh, God, I'm sorry – it's *your* party . . .'

'Anne? Oh, we're in the middle of a divorce! Ha ha! JOKE!'

'She's been up to her eyes with work lately.'

'Don't worry, I've got a late pass!'

'She's at a seminar with the Congolese football team.'

'Anne? Anne who? Anne Marronnier? That's weird, she's got the same surname as me!'

'Anne's in hospital . . . a terrible accident . . . she begged me to stay with her, but I really didn't want to miss the party. This salmon roe is divine, isn't it?'

'The way I look at it is, if she keeps on working like this, I'll soon be filthy rich.'

'Marriage is an institution, but it's not perfect.'

'Where's Alice? Do you know Alice? You haven't seen Alice, have you? Is Alice coming?'

On the other hand, whenever I heard someone say Alice's name, it was like a knife through the heart.

'Dear friends,

Would you be so good as never to mention that name again in my presence?

Many thanks,

Me'

Heaven is other people, but sometimes they overstep the mark. Everywhere I went, people were gossiping about me and Alice. I didn't care that they were gossiping about me, people have been spreading vile rumours about me since before they were true. The jaded, world-weary carping of my friends had never bothered me before, but when they started running Alice down I was, well, I was almost shocked. I went out at night to make life last longer. I just couldn't bear the thought of life ending at eight o'clock every night. I wanted to steal the hours being wasted by sensible people who went to bed early. But I wasn't prepared to put up with this. I wouldn't go out any more. It finally sunk in that I hated these vultures who fed on other people's misery. Once I had been a vulture, but no longer. Suddenly, I didn't find them entertaining any more. For once I wanted to make a go of things; for once I wanted to seize my chance. The vultures would have to carry on without me. I gave up writing gossip columns for the society pages of glossy magazines.

Farewell my fair-weather society friends, I will not miss you, you will carry on festering without me. I don't envy you, I pity you. And that is the tragedy of contemporary society: no one envies the rich any more. They have become fat, ugly, vulgar, the women are nipped and tucked, the men are doing time, the kids are doing drugs. They have no taste. They pose for photo shoots in *Hello!* The rich have forgotten that money is a means, not an end. They don't know what to do with money any more. At least the poor can dream that if only they had money, they would be happy. The rich have no excuses, they can hardly pretend that if only they had another country house, another sports car, another pair of thousand-dollar shoes, another super-model on their arm, they would be happy. Millionaires take Prozac, because nobody dreams of being like them any more, not even them.

Writing gossip columns about the nightlife of Paris had become a catch-22. I would go out and get hammered so I could write a column about going out and getting shit-faced. I would no longer be a creature of the night, now I would have to face the day. What sort of column could an unemployed parasite write? Think Count Dracula in broad daylight, how would he make ends meet? What kind of job would a bloodsucker be good at?

And that's how I became a literary critic.

# XXXIV

# The Theory of Eternal Return

When I tell my parents (divorced since 1972) that Anne and I have separated, they try to talk me round: 'Are you sure this is what you want?' 'Maybe you can get back together,' 'Don't do anything rash . . .' The sixties' obsession with psychoanalysis probably explains why my parents are convinced this is their fault. They are much more worried than I am. Suddenly I don't feel that I can mention Alice. One catastrophe at a time is enough for them to deal with. Calmly, I explain that love lasts three years. For completely different reasons they both disagree, but their arguments are not very convincing. After all, their marriage didn't last much longer than mine. I'm surprised to realise that they are trying to relive their own lives through me. I can't believe that my parents invested so much time hoping, thinking and finally believing that I would be different.

Children exist to make the same mistakes our parents made, in precisely the same order, just as once they made the mistakes their parents made, and so on. But that doesn't matter. It is better than constantly making the same mistakes you made before. Which is what I do.

I wind up in the same rut every three years. My life is in a constant state of *déjà vu*, a series of reruns. It's as if I'm a CD player programmed to endlessly repeat the same song. (I like comparing myself to machines, because machines are easy to fix.) But this is not the comedy of repetition, it is an all too real nightmare. Imagining yourself on a white-knuckle roller-coaster with stomach-churning corkscrews and heart-stopping plunges. Although the ride is exhilarating, once is enough. You step off and yell 'Jesus Christ, you won't get me on that thing again, I nearly spewed my guts three times!' Me, I get on that thing again and again. I have a season ticket. Space Mountain is a place I call home.

I finally understand what Camus meant when he wrote: 'One must imagine Sisyphus happy.' He meant that maybe we spend our whole lives making the same mistakes, but maybe that's what happiness is. I have to cling to that hope. I must learn to love my unhappiness for the thrill-packed ride it is.

A dream: I'm rolling my rock up the boulevard Saint-Germain. I double-park it. A cop stops me and tells me that if I don't move the rock, he'll have to give me a ticket. I'm trying to move the rock when suddenly it rolls away down the rue Saint-Benoît, picking up speed as it goes. I can't control it: hardly surprising since it is a 6-ton block of granite. At the corner of the rue Jacob, it smashes into a little convertible, crushing the bonnet, the driver's door and the pretty boy who was driving. I stand next to his sexy, grief-stricken widow and fill out the accident report. I nibble the nape of her neck. Where it says REGISTRATION, I write 'S.I.S.Y.P.H.U.S.' (secondhand). Then inch by inch, I roll my rock back up the rue Bonaparte, and leave it in the car park at Saint-Germain-des-Prés. Tomorrow, the whole circus will begin again. And one must imagine me happy.

# XXXV

# Tender is the Night

Since I decided not to have anything more to do with Paris nightlife, I've been going out every night – I mean, we have to say our goodbyes. It starts to get around that I'm single. In Paris, a young, single omnisexual is as hard to find as a tramp in the lobby of the Gstaad Palace Hotel. Nobody seems to notice that I'm wasting away, which is hardly surprising since I was pretty skinny even when I was happy. I mooch around the city with my despair slung over my shoulder. Tonight, Alice dumped me, she told me she couldn't go on lying to her husband. She usually dumps me on Fridays so she can have a guilt-free weekend and phones me up on Monday afternoon. So I phoned Jean-Georges to tell him I was coming to his dinner party and asked if he wanted me to bring a bottle of wine, or something for dessert.

I have decided to cheat on Alice with her best friend. I phone Julie and invite her to the dinner party. She didn't take much persuading. I told her I was in a really bad way: women, I've discovered, can never resist it when their best friend's boyfriend tells them he's in a bad way. It brings out their maternal side, awakens the latent nurse, the Little Sister of the Poor.

Julie's problem is she is stunningly sexy. She's always complaining that guys never fall in love with her. And it is true that as soon as they meet her men have a depressing tendency to want to perform a breast exam, or indeed a complete physical. Men do not respect Julie, but it's partly her own fault – no one forces her to wear T-shirts designed for an eight-year-old that barely come down to her pierced belly button.

'You know, if you don't sleep with a man straight away, he will eventually fall in love with you. Guys are like cheap cuts of meat, you have to let them stew.'

'So you're saying I should treat men the way Alice treats you?'

Not so blonde, our Julie.

'On second thoughts, be gentle with them, take pity on them, guys are sensitive creatures at heart.'

Jean-Georges' parties are always perfect. Here, sensitive souls may converse in perfect harmony. Belligerence of any kind is forbidden, though his parties are always packed with celebrities – actors, directors, fashion designers, painters and even people who don't yet realise they're artists. I've noticed that the more talented people are, the gentler they are. It's axiomatic. Julie and I are sitting on a sofa, nibbling canapés.

'How long have you known Jean-Georges?' she asks.

'Since forever. Don't be fooled by the fact that we probably won't say two words to each other tonight. He's my best friend – in fact, he's one of the only people of my own gender I can stand to be with. We're like a couple of elderly queers who don't sleep together.'

'So,' she whispers, sitting up suddenly which brings me nose to tip with her erect nipples, 'are you going to tell me what's wrong?'

'Alice left me, my wife left me, and my grandmother's just died. I never thought I could feel so alone.'

As I beweep my outcast fate, I edge closer to her. At parties, the art of seduction is simply a process of closing the gap. Inch by inch, careful not to be too obvious, you move closer. If you spot a girl you fancy, walk over to her (about 6 feet away). If she still looks attractive at this distance, start a conversation (3 feet). If she laughs at your feeble jokes, ask her to dance, or offer her a drink (18 inches). Sit next to her (12 inches). As soon as you see a gleam in her eyes, gently push that stray lock of hair behind her ear (6 inches). If she doesn't protest, talk to her a little more (3 inches). If her breathing becomes heavy, press your lips to hers (0 inches). The ultimate objective is to narrow the distance between you to a negative value equal to penetration (the national average is 6.6 inches).

'I'm as miserable as a black, black stone,' I say, narrowing the distance that separates me from the point of no return. 'Worse, actually, since a stone doesn't feel any pain, a stone doesn't die.'

'Yeah, that's tough . . . so, pretty bummed then?'

I'm beginning to wonder what Alice sees in this beautiful airhead. I must have misunderstood, this woman can't be Alice's best friend. But I keep up my patter.

'I suppose . . . I suppose I've only myself to blame. Writers are never happy . . .'

'I suppose. Oh, you mean you're a writer? D'you write books and stuff? I thought you were an events organiser.'

'Well, yes, that too. But, without wanting to boast, I have published a couple of things recently.' I look down at my nails. '*Journey to the End of the Shite*, maybe you've heard of it?'

'Um . . .'

'Well, I wrote that. I also wrote *The Unbearable Shiteness of Being*, and at the moment I'm working on *The Sorrows of Young Wanker* . . .'

'So, what's the next event you're organising? Can you put me on the guest list?'

Some girls are so bovine they make you feel like a country vet. But I have to keep going. If I start dating Julie, Alice will be devastated. I have to keep trying.

'You know the best thing about being divorced, Julie? Being able to wash your hands without getting soap stuck to your fingers . . .'

'I don't get it.'

'Because of the wedding ring.'

'Oh, right, now I get it . . . You're funny.'

'So, are you seeing anyone at the moment?'

'No. Well, I mean, yeah, a couple of guys. Nothing serious.'

'Same as me.'

'No, you're in love with Alice.'

'Yeah, but it's complicated. My problem is that I fall in love but I can't manage to stay in love.'

As I say these words, I am precisely 1 millimetre from her bee-stung lips, trying to decide if she's had collagen injections. I'm about to move in for the kill when she turns her cheek to me. The brush-off.

That's it, I can't stand it any more. I walk away, abandoning her on the sofa. Poor bitch, I can see why guys treat her like a disposable razor. Let's face it, Alice wouldn't care even if I fucked Julie right in front of her (she'd probably find it a turn-on). I love you, Alice, no one but you, it's something you have to accept, even if you're not prepared to turn your life around. Whether you like it or not, somewhere nearby there will always be a man who loves you and suffers for your love. Reminding you of this is the only hope I have of one day winning your heart. I'll be a long-suffering lover, a mute reproach, a silent temptation. Call me Tantalus.

A couple of hours later, I was in the kitchen leafing through a dog-eared copy of *Tender is the Night*, Julie was flirting with a father and his son, triggering a furious family feud. I spent the weekend getting completely shit-faced. I spent three days in Jean-Georges' place surviving entirely on Pringles and Four Roses whisky. The only thing we listened to was The Beatles' 'Rubber Soul'. At some point I think I remember Julien composing a song at the piano. I staggered to my feet every three hours only so I could carry on drinking, because, though it's a cliché, the best way to avoid remorse is to forget anything ever happened.

# XXXVI

# Freelance

I set up as a freelance journalist. It keeps me busy. I fill the waste-land of my soul with meaningless work. As a result, I'm asked to do a pitch for a new perfume – 'Hypnosis, by David Copper-field, Las Vegas'. The pitch is worth fifty grand (twenty-five if we don't get the contract). I need to find a phrase, something short, punchy and provocative which simultaneously gets across the USP while also making clear the value-add. The Unique Selling Proposition being that this perfume, thanks to its secret formulation, enables women (the target) to seduce men (the target's target) not just for the night, but for a lifetime of enduring love. A week later, I go back with the following list of slogans:

*You don't need a wedding ring when you wear Hypnosis by Copperfield.*

*Hypnosis by Copperfield: no tricks, just magic.*

*Hypnosis by Copperfield: for tonight, and every night.*

*Hypnosis by Copperfield: every secret compartment hides a love story.*

*Spray on Hypnosis, and watch it change your life.*

*Hypnosis by Copperfield. The genie in the bottle.*

*Hypnosis: the scent of amnesia.*

*Hypnosis by Copperfield. Afterwards, you'll pretend you can't remember.*

The meeting is a disaster. No one likes the pitch, not even me. I listen to what they have to say. The same afternoon, I head for Verbier, a Swiss winter sports resort in Valais. It is from here that, after three weeks of effort, I fax back the slogan you all know, the slogan which, in less than a year, was to make Hypnosis the market leader in mass-market fragrances.

*HYPNOSIS BY COPPERFIELD. BECAUSE WITHOUT IT, LOVE LASTS THREE YEARS.*

# XXXVII

# The Romantic Cynic

Here I sit in the same café where I sit every night, trying to think of a solution. Though I've tried to convince myself that I'm dead, all available evidence suggests I'm still alive. There were a couple of close calls: I was nearly killed in a hit-and-run (I crossed the road in time), fell out of a window (I landed in some bushes), nearly contracted a deadly virus (I wore a condom). It's a pity. Death becomes me. Before my descent into Hades, I was afraid of death; now, I would welcome it as a release. I don't understand why people are worried about dying. At least death holds more surprises than life. Now, I'm looking forward to dying, I'll be happy to leave this miserable world and finally find out what happens in the next. People who are afraid of dying have no sense of adventure.

My problem is that you are the solution. Cynics and pessimists are always the most hopeless romantics: it appeals to our temperament. I spent my life desperately hoping my cynicism would be refuted. It is those who do not believe that love exists who most need it: at heart, every Valmont is a romantic just itching to get out his lute.

The trap snaps shut again, and once more I find myself caught up in its infernal machinations, suddenly dreaming of dappled gardens in country houses, of the song of the rain on a roof at twilight. Suddenly I feel the urge to gather a bouquet of violets, to be far from the city, alone with Alice so that we can make love again and again until finally we burst with joy, sob with pleasure, hold each other close, comforted by the fact that we are the perfect match, chilled melon and Parma ham, or Florence or Milan if there's time . . .

# XXXVIII

# Letters (III)

Fourth letter to Alice:

Dear Ostrich,

I think about you all the time. I think of you as I walk through the morning frost, walking slowly so that I have more time to think of you. I think of you at night, at every party. And at every party I drink to forget you and it only seems to make me remember. I think about you when we're together and when we're apart. I try to think of ways not to think of you, but I can't seem to. If you have any tips on how to forget you, let me know.

This has been the worst weekend of my life. I have never missed anyone as I miss you. Without you, my life is a hospital waiting-room with harsh fluorescent lights and peeling lino on the floor. What you are doing to me is inhumane. The worst thing is that even in my waiting-room, I'm all alone: there are no walking wounded, no bleeding hearts to reassure me; no magazines on the coffee-table to take my mind off things, no numbered ticket which might allow me to hope that one day my wait will end. My stomach aches, and there's no one to nurse me better. Love is an ache in the pit of my stomach, and you are the only cure.

Alice. Never did I imagine how much that name would come to mean to me. I had heard of suffering, but I did not know its name was Alice. Alice, I love you. Your name isn't Alice, it's Alice-I-love-you.

Your (deeply depressed) Marc

Alice phoned me, on cue, on Monday afternoon and told me she was crazy about me, promised she would never leave me again. We borrowed a friend's apartment where I tenderly undressed her. To say our reconciliation was pleasurable would be an understatement. The hours we spent together that afternoon should be filed as the benchmark in Sèvres under 'exceptional sexual pleasure as experienced between a human couple of complementary genders'. And then, in spite of the promises she had made to me, Alice, exhausted, went home to her husband at nine o'clock, leaving me alone to face the empty hours.

# XXXIX

## Still Falling

I should warn you: I don't know whether this book will have a happy ending. The past few weeks have been among the most miserable and the most magnificent I have ever experienced, and I have no reason to think that things won't go on like this. I have tried to shape my destiny, but destiny isn't Plasticine.

Last week, my world came to an end. Alice phoned and told me that she and Antoine were going on holiday together to try and save their marriage. This time, she said, it really was over between us. We hung up without saying goodbye. *Hiroshima mon amour.* You see what happens when you fall in love? Before you know it, you're quoting Marguerite Duras.

I watch a fly bashing its head against my bedroom window and I realise that, like me, between the fly and reality there is a pane of glass.

You're never alone with a schizophrenic. Alice has her cake and gets to eat it, too – with me she has her forbidden passion, and still she has her cosy little life with Antoine. Why settle for one life when you can have two? Alice zaps between men as if we were cable channels (I just hope I'm Eurosport).

It's over. I.T.S. O.V.E.R. I'm surprised I am capable of writing these words when I'm utterly incapable of believing them. I have flashes of egotism, when I try to convince myself that if she doesn't love me any more, then I don't love her! You can't stand the heat? Too bad, bitch! But these flashes of self-respect are short-lived, since I have an underdeveloped will to live.

I'm afraid you'll have to forgive me. Writers are a miserable bunch. I hope my suffering isn't boring you. All writing is a form of complaint. There's not much difference between a novel and a Post Office complaints form. If I had a choice, I wouldn't spend my time holed up in this flat, typing. But I have no choice.

What's wrong with me? . . . I'm writing the same book everyone else writes. A tale of star-crossed lovers . . . You leave the wife who loves you for a woman who doesn't . . . Where are the shamelessly debauched soirées? Why am I suddenly writing about the sentimental problems of Left Bank lovers . . .? It's like new French cinema: let's make a film about the problems of people who haven't got any problems . . . And yet, for the first time in my life, I feel an overwhelming physical *need* to write. In the past, when writers talked about their *need* to write, I nodded sagely, but I had no idea what they were talking about . . . Even this pathetic attempt at self-deprecation is just self-defence to the nth power . . . (Thank you, Drieu. Thank you, Nourissier.) I can't bring myself to write about anything else . . . It is something I had to write someday . . . Until you've written your divorce novel, you haven't written . . . Maybe it's not such a bad idea, taking the personal and making it general . . . If my experience is banal, it is universal . . . It's important to avoid originality and stick to subjects that are timeless . . . I'm bored with post-modernism . . . This is my apprenticeship in sincerity . . . I know that somewhere beneath all this suffering is a flowing river. If I can find its source, perhaps it might be of some comfort to the 'happy few' who have known despair like this. I want to warn them, to explain things, so that they may never know the pain I feel. This is the task I have set myself, and it helps me see things more clearly. But it is possible that this river is a subterranean stream which never surfaces . . .

# XL

# Conversation in a Palace

Jean-Georges has never seen me like this. He tries desperately to cheer me up, like someone offering a hand to a drowning man. We are sitting in a bar in some flash hotel, but I don't remember which one, we've trawled them all. I ask him:

'Do you think love lasts three years?'

He looks at me derisively.

'Three years? That's optimistic! My God, three days is more than enough! Who has been filling your head with such nonsense, poppet?'

'It's something to do with hormones, apparently, or body chemistry or something . . . After three years, that's it, you can't love any more. Don't you think that's depressing?'

'No, poppet, I don't. Love lasts as long as it lasts, it doesn't matter to me. But if you want it to last, you need to learn to cope with boredom. You need to find someone you long to be bored stiff with. If you can't have undying passion, you might as well settle for pleasurable tedium.'

'Maybe you're right . . . Do you think I'll ever end up chasing after something that isn't there?'

'Yes, poppet. But you're looking at it arse-backwards. The more desperately you try to find love, the more gutted you are when things go wrong. What you should do is try to find boredom, you'll be surprised how often you're not bored. It's impossible to plan for love: boredom is the natural state of man, love is the cherry on top. Remember: fear of boredom . . .'

'. . . is the first sign of self-loathing . . . I know, you've told me. You know, when I look at all the couples I know who despise each other, bore each other, cheat on each other and stay together for the sake of the marriage, I'm glad I got divorced . . . At least my memories are happy ones.'

'Ah, my sweet and tender hooligan, but I wasn't talking about Anne, I was talking about Alice. Here you are fantasising about Alice when you don't even know her. This is your problem: you fall in love with people you don't know. I'm not sure you'd be able to put up with her if you had to live with her. What turns you on is the fact that you can't be together. If I were you, I'd phone Anne.'

'Jean-Georges?'

'Yes, my little chickadee?'

'Don't talk shit. D'you fancy another drink?'

'Okay, but it's your shout.'

'Jean-Georges, can I ask you something?'

'Fire away.'

'Have you ever had your heart broken?'

'You know perfectly well I haven't. I've never been in love, it is my one great tragedy.'

'I envy you. I fall in love but I can't STAY in love, which is much worse.'

Jean-Georges is silent and suddenly I regret what I've said. He turns away, his eyes mist over. His voice is serious now:

'Don't try and turn things round. You know perfectly well I envy you, I always have. I've been suffering since the day I was born. You are only just discovering a pain that I would give anything to feel. Do you mind if we change the subject?'

There you go. Misery loves company. Now we're both depressed. Fat lot of good that's done us.

'Do you think I'm a bastard?'

'No, of course not. You're an apprentice bastard, you're an amateur, my little mouse. You have a lot to learn. On the other hand . . .'

'On the other hand what?'

'On the other hand, you're a fudge-packing bumboy and if you don't shut up I'm going to stick it where the sun don't shine.'

And with that the filthy slob grabs me and we roll onto the floor, knocking over the table, the drinks, the chairs in a fit of laughter, while the barman frantically flips through the phone book to find an emergency number for the Sainte-Anne Psychiatric Unit.

# XLI

# Conjectures

It was at this point that something terrible happened: I started leaving my socks on when I went to bed. I had to do something fast before I started drinking my own urine. That night I tossed and turned, thinking about what Jean-Georges had said. Maybe he was right, maybe I should phone Anne. After all, since Alice didn't want me, maybe the divorce was a mistake. Perhaps all was not lost: lots of people get divorced and fall in love with each other again. Look at Adeline and Johnny Hallyday. Bad example. Liz Taylor and Richard Burton. No, not much better.

I could get Anne back. I had to get Anne back. I had to put things right. We never really tried before, now we would try everything. We were so busy tiptoeing around trying to be understanding that we'd never really talked about things. Anne and I would get back together, and one day we'd look back on our divorce and laugh. We'd come through worse things.

Actually, we hadn't come through worse things. Once upon a time, if you had a fling, your marriage would survive it. Nowadays, a marriage is just a fling. We live in a society based on selfishness. Sociologists refer to this as the Individualistic Society, but there's a simpler way of putting it: we live in a society of solitude. Nowadays, there are no families, no villages, no God. Our forefathers delivered us of these oppressions and in their stead, they turned on the TV. Left to our own devices, we are incapable of taking an interest in anything but our own navels.

Nonetheless, I devised a cunning plan. I had hoped not to be driven to such extreme measures, but Alice going away with Antoine called for a counterstrike of nuclear proportions. There was no room for dignity here. My plan was to call Anne. With a smile I wish were Machiavellian, but is actually just intimidated, I pick up the phone.

# XLII

# The Cunning Plan

'How long has it been?' I ask Anne, pulling out the table so she can sit on the bench. There was a time when we always liked to sit side by side in restaurants, but that was then; tonight, we're sitting opposite each other.

She looks at me curiously and then says:

'Four months, one week, three days, eight hours and [she checks her watch before finishing] sixteen minutes.'

'And forty-three, forty-four, forty-five seconds . . .'

At first, we make polite conversation, we talk about anything but why we're here: her job, my job, mutual friends, shared memories. We chat as if none of this had ever happened. But Anne can tell that I'm miserable, and then she feels miserable because she's not the cause of my misery. By the time we get to dessert, she's angry and spoiling for a fight:

'Look, you didn't invite me to dinner to talk about old times. What do you want?'

'Well . . . There's some stuff of yours at my place and I thought maybe you could come round and pick it up. And while you were there, I thought maybe we could go away for the weekend together and try to save our marriage . . .'

'Are you out of your mind? We're divorced, Marc! I know

perfectly well that it's not me you're in love with, I'm not some fucking doll you can drop and pick up.'

'Shh . . . not so loud.'

I turn to the guy at the next table.

'We're divorced, I asked her to go away with me for the weekend and she knocked me back, okay? Now you know everything. So you can stop eavesdropping, or maybe life with that tart you're having dinner with is so pathetic that you have to pry into other people's lives.'

The guy at the next table gets up, I get up, eventually the women prise us apart, so at least you can't say there's no action in this book. I pay the bill and we leave the restaurant. Outside, it's even darker than before. We walk for a bit, laughing. I say I'm sorry. She says it's okay. She's coping with our divorce better than I am.

'It's too late, Marc. It's too late. I'm in love with someone else, and so are you: it's over.'

'I know, I know, I'm being silly . . . I just thought maybe we could give it another try . . . You sure you don't want me to give you a lift home?'

'No, it's okay, I'll get a cab. Look, Marc, I'd like to give you a bit of advice. In future, when you're dating a woman, learn to empathise, learn to see things through her eyes.'

And then, just as we are about to go our separate ways, things get emotional. We are both fighting back tears, but in our hearts they trickle down. I realise I will never hear Anne's childlike laugh again. My loss is her new boyfriend's gain, if he knows how to make her laugh. Anne is a stranger now. She steps into the taxi, I softly close the door behind her. She smiles at me through the rear windscreen and the taxi pulls away . . . If this were a movie, I would run through the rain and catch up with the taxi at the next set of traffic lights and we would fall into each other's arms. Or Anne would suddenly change her mind, like Audrey Hepburn in *Breakfast at Tiffany's*, and tell the driver to stop. But this isn't a movie, and in real life, taxis just keep moving.

We leave home and leave our parents behind only to leave home and leave our first wife behind, but the pain is the same; suddenly we feel orphaned.

# XLIII

# A Cheap Trick

Married couples have dinner, lovers have lunch. The next time you see a couple in a little bistro having lunch, try taking a photo – they'll bite your head off. Try the same thing with a couple having dinner and they will smile and pose for the camera.

As soon as she got back from her conjugal weekend away, Alice phoned me. After I had dutifully empathised with her, seen the world through her eyes, imagined what she must be going through, I coolly suggested we have lunch.

'I'll bring a slide projector.'

She didn't think this was funny, which was just as well since I wasn't trying to be funny. As soon as she arrives, she tells me the trip was a disaster, swears that she and Antoine didn't sleep together, but I cut her off:

'It's okay, don't worry. Anne and I are going away this weekend to try to save our marriage.'

This is a lie. Everyone knows this is a lie, everyone except Alice, who looks as if she's had a Scud missile in the face.

'Oh.'

'So,' I say, picking up the conversation effortlessly, 'how was the holiday?'

Alice slaps me, but strangely she's the one who bursts into

tears. I've been collecting melodramatic meals recently. Fortunately, the couple at the next table have just left. Unfortunately, Alice leaves too. The restaurant feels a bit empty. And while I try to savour my revenge, 'here I am alone with a heart full of alms' (Paul Morand). So I return to drinking hectolitres of wine until I can't stand up straight, nor indeed sit. Another liquid lunch. Revenge is a dish best not served at all.

The strange thing is not the fact that all the world's a stage, it's the fact that there are so few people in the cast.

# XLIV

# Letters (IV)

## *A week later*

Last letter to Alice :

My love,

The weekend with Anne was a disaster. I can't bring myself to talk about it. I needed to know, I needed to be sure that I'd made the right decision. I'm sorry if I hurt you, though maybe part of me wanted you to realise how much you hurt me. I know that's stupid, because you can never know how much you hurt me.

Alice, we were made for each other. It's terrifying. When I'm with you, everything is beautiful, even me. But because you're afraid, I'm afraid. I can't bear the fact that I'm not the only man in your life. I hate your past, because it stands in the way of my future.

I wish there was some point to all this pain. Why don't you trust me? Because I'm crazy? You can hardly accuse me of that, since you're crazy too. Do you really think we only love each other because things are complicated? If you do, then maybe we should finish it. I'd rather be miserable without you than miserable with you.

Our love is indelible, I can't understand why you can't see that. I am your future. I'm here. I'm real. You can't just keep pretending that I don't exist. I'm sorry but, in the words of Leonard Cohen, 'I'm Your Man'.

We have no right to run away from happiness. Most people aren't as lucky as we are. When they fancy each other, they don't fall in love. When they fall in love, things are lousy in bed. Or if things are fantastic in bed, they have nothing to talk about afterwards. We have got everything, except we have nothing because we're not together.

What we're doing is unforgivable. Let's stop making each other miserable. When you finally get a chance to be happy, it's a crime not to jump at the chance. We're being cruel to ourselves. How much longer can we go on like this? Putting ourselves and everyone else through all this pain is immoral, and for nothing. No one will blame us if we seize this opportunity.

This time, this really will be my last letter. I can't go on playing cat and mouse. I'm worn out, I'm washed up, I'm lying at your feet just waiting for you to finish me off. There comes a point when you hurt so much that you lose all sense of pride. I'm not writing to ask you to come back, I'm just writing to tell you I'll always be here waiting. One word from you, and we'll start that ostrich farm. No word, and I'll still be here, somewhere, stalking the same planet, waiting for you. I love you beyond anything I can write, I want only you, I think only of you, body and soul, I belong only to you.

Marc, who cried while he wrote this.

# XLV

## So

So, I pick up my pen to put into words how much I love her, how she has the longest hair in the world and how I'm drowning in it, and if you think that's pathetic, I pity you, how her eyes are mine and she is mine and she is me and when she screams, I scream and everything I will ever do will be for her, always and always I will give her everything, and from now until the day I die I will get up in the morning only for her, only to make her want to love me and to kiss me again and again, her wrists, her shoulders, her breasts and it is here that I realise that when you're in love you write sentences that have no end, there is no time to put a full stop, you have to write and write and run faster than your heart, and the sentence doesn't want to end, love knows no punctuation, tears of passion trickle down, when you're in love you wind up writing everlasting things, when you're in love suddenly you think you're Albert Cohen, Alice came back, Alice left Antoine, she left, at last, at last, and together we flew away, literally and metaphorically, we caught the first flight to Rome, where else, the Hotel d'Angleterre, the Piazza Navona, the Trevi Fountain, vows of undying love, riding around on a Vespa, when we asked for crash-helmets the rental guy took one look at us and realised and said don't worry, it's too hot for helmets, and love, love uninterrupted, three, four, five times a day, your cock hurts, you've never come so much and then you start all over and you're not alone any more, the sky is pink, without you I was nothing, now at last I can breathe, we walk on air, hovering a few inches above the pavement, no one notices but us, we are on cushions of air, we smile for no reason at the citizens of Rome who think we're simple-minded, or members of some bizarre cult, the Sect of Those who Smile and Levitate, suddenly everything is easy, you put one foot in front of the other and it's happiness love life tomato and mozzarella salad drenched in olive oil and pasta parmigiano and we never finish what's on our plates, too busy gazing into each other's eyes, stroking each other's horny hands, I don't think we slept a wink in ten days, ten months, ten years, ten centuries, the sun over the beach at Fregene we take Polaroids like the one that Anne found in Rio, it's enough just to look at you and breathe, this is forever, forever and always, it's incredible, astonishing how choked up with happiness we are, I've never experienced anything like this, do you feel what I feel, you could never love me as much as I love you, no I love you more, no me, me, okay it's us, it's so wonderful to suddenly be so weak, to run towards the sea, you were made for me, how can I begin to describe what it is with words, it's as though you've stepped from the dead of night into the glittering daylight, like the endless rush of coming up on Ecstasy, like a pain in your belly suddenly going away, like the first gulp of air when you've been holding your breath underwater, like a single answer to every question. Days fly by like minutes, you forget everything, you are reborn with every second, you think no ugly thoughts, you are in a constant now that is sensual, sexual, wondrous, invincible, nothing can touch us, we know that our love is strong enough to save the world, we are horrifyingly happy, you go up to the room, wait for me in the lobby

I'll be right down, and as soon as the lift doors close I take the stairs four at a time and open the lift door for you, almost crying from the three minutes we have spent apart, when you bit into a ripe peach and juice trickled onto your thighs, oh fuck I want you all the time, again and again, look I'm coming on your face, oh Marc, oh Alice, oh God I'm coming, we didn't spend a single minute sightseeing, that's it, now she's got the giggles, what did I say to make you laugh like that, it's just nerves, I came so hard, I love you, I love you, what day is it?

# II

# THREE YEARS LATER
# IN FORMENTERA

# I

# D-Day −7

Casa le Moult. Here I am in Formentera to finish this novel. This is the last one of the trilogy (in volume one I fell in love; in the second, I got married; in the third I got divorced and fell in love again. The wheel has come full circle). You do your best to innovate, to stretch the medium (weird words, Anglicisms, odd sentence structures, advertising copy, etc.) and the message (clubbing, sex, rock and roll . . .), but you quickly realise that all you want to do is write a love story in simple sentences – the most difficult thing in the world to do.

I listen to the sea. Finally I start to slow down. Speed makes it impossible to be yourself. Here, you can read the length of the days on the sky. In Paris, my life has no sky. Churn out slogans, fax advertising copy, answer the phone, quick, late for a meeting, lunch at the desk, quick, quick, take the scooter, nip through the traffic, show up late for some cocktail party. I needed to slam on the brakes. Focus. Do one thing at a time. Touch the beauty of silence. Enjoy the slowness. Listen to the perfume of colours. All those things the world would like to take away.

We need to start again. Society needs to be built again from the ground up. Nowadays, those who have money have no time and those who have time have no money. Escaping from work is as difficult as escaping unemployment. The idler is public enemy number one. You chain people with money: they give up their freedom just to be able to pay their taxes. Let's not beat around the bush: the real issue in the next century will be how to eliminate the tyranny of business.

Formentera is a tiny island ... A satellite of Ibiza in the constellation of the Balearics. Formentera is like Corsica without the bombs, Ibiza without the clubs, Mustique without Mick Jagger, Capri without Hervé Vilard, the Basque country without the rain.

White sunlight. Spin on a Vespa. Heat and dust. Withered flowers. Turquoise sea. Smell of pine. Song of cicadas. Yellow-bellied lizards. Goats gently butting.

'No buts,' I tell them.

Red sun. *Gambas a la plancha. Vamos a la playa.* Stars in the sky. Gin gimlet. I was searching for relief, here, where the heat makes it impossible to write long sentences. Perhaps coma is not the only place to holiday. The sea is full of water. The sky is moving constantly. The stars are shooting. Breathing is a full-time occupation.

It's the story of a guy who holes up on an island to finish this book. This guy leads a hectic life and finds it weird to be all alone in the middle of nowhere with no phone and no TV. In Paris, he's dynamic, he's a go-getter; here, he barely moves. He models himself on Barnabooth in Florence, Byron in Venice, the panda in Vincennes zoo. The only time he speaks is to say hello to the San Francescos' maid. This guy wears a black shirt, white jeans and Tod's sandals. Drinks only Pernod and gin gimlets. Eats only crisps and nachos. Listens to only one record: Arthur Rubinstein playing the 'Kreutzer' Sonata. Yesterday, you might have spotted him cheering a goal in the France–Spain match, a courageous gesture, but in poor taste when you're the only French guy in a harbour bar in Spain. If you ran into him, you'd probably think: 'What the fuck is this Parisian jerk doing in La Fonda Pepe in the off-season?' Which would piss me off somewhat, given that I'm the guy in question. So, put a sock in it, okay? I am a hermit smiling at the warm west wind.

In precisely one week, Alice and I will have been together three years.

# II

# D-Day −6

Okay, so, when Alice walked out on Antoine and afterwards, when we moved in together on the rue Mazarin (where Antoine Blondin died), I admit that I freaked out a bit. Happiness is a lot more frightening than depression. Finally having everything I ever wanted filled me with joy, but at the same time made me wonder. Would I make the same mistakes again? What if I was just a serial romantic? Now I had Alice, did I really want her? Would I become a pushover? Would I get bored of her? When would I stop asking myself these stupid questions, for fuck's sake?

Antoine wanted to kill me, to kill her, to kill himself. Our relationship rose from the ashes of a double divorce, as though it required two human sacrifices to create one new love. It's what Schumpeter called 'creative destruction', though Schumpeter was an economist and in general they're not romantics. We had destroyed two marriages in order to be together, like The Blob absorbing its victims so that it can grow. Happiness is a monstrous beast that, if it does not kill you, will force you to undertake at least a few murders.

Jean-Georges came to stay with me in Formentera. Together we put the world to rights and then go snorkelling and visit the fish. He's writing a play, so he's drinking as heavily as I am.

Poem to be read while drunk:

> *On the isle of Formentera*
> *I came down with liver failure*

We meet stoned couples of ageing hippies who've been living here since the sixties. How have they managed to stay together all this time? It almost makes me cry. I buy dope for them. Jean-Georges and I get pissed and play pool in small cafés. He's just met the love of his life, for the first time in his life, he's happy.

'Love: what else is there to live for?'

'Are you going to have kids?'

'No way! Bring a child into a world as fucked-up as this? That would be criminal, selfish, narcissistic!'

'I give a woman something better than a kid, I give her a book,' I declared, raising my finger.

We give the waitress a wink. She's stunning, wearing a bolero, a light down covers her dusky skin, she has large dark eyes, arches her back, wild as a squaw.

'She looks like Alice,' I say. 'That means if I sleep with her, I haven't been unfaithful.'

Alice is still in Paris, she's coming out to join me here next week.

In six days I will have been living with her for three years.

# III

# D-Day −5

The waitress with the backless dress is called Matilda. She's so hot. Jean-Georges sang her a Harry Belafonte song:
*Matilda, she take me money and run Venezuela.*

I think I could fall in love with her if I didn't miss Alice so much. In the bar at Ses Roques, we asked her to dance. Her bronzed hands clapped to the beat, she shimmied her hips, her hair whipped round her like a tornado. She had hair in her armpits. Jean-Georges asked her:

'Excuse me, Señorita, we need a place to sleep. Have you got any space in your house, *por favor*?'

She was wearing a fine gold chain around her waist, and another round her ankle. Unfortunately, Matilda didn't take our money and run off to Venezuela. She was happy to sit with us rolling spliffs until we fell asleep beneath the stars. Her fingers were long and nimble. She licked the cigarette paper meticulously. I think we all felt a little troubled, even her.

Back at the Casa, completely shit-faced, Matilda grabbed my cock. She had a cavernous but very muscular pussy that smelled of holidays. Her hair stank of sinsemilla. She screamed so loudly that Jean-Georges had to put something in her mouth to shut her up; after that we swapped places before ejaculating at the same time over her large firm breasts. Just after I came, I woke up sweating, dying of thirst. A true hermit does not abuse narcotic plants.

In five days I will have been living with Alice for three years.

# IV

# D-Day −4

The single man reverts to the Neanderthal: after only a few days, he no longer shaves or washes, he begins to grunt. It required millions of years to bring mankind to this civilisation, but less than a week for a man to revert to homo erectus. My gait is increasingly simian, I scratch my testicles, eat my snot and move in short hops. At mealtimes, I mash everything up together and eat with my hands: sausages and chewing-gum, cheese and onion crisps and chocolate milk, Coca-Cola and wine. Afterwards, I burp, fart and snore. This is what it means to be a young avant-garde French writer today.

Alice showed up unexpectedly. Three days before she was due to arrive, she crept up behind me in El Mercado de la Mola and put her hands over my eyes:

'Guess who?'

'*No sé*. Matilda?'

'Bastard!'

'Alice!'

We threw our arms round each other.

'Well, if you were hoping to surprise me, you surprised me!'

Did I have to say that?

'Admit it, you weren't expecting me. And who the hell is Matilda?'

'Oh, no one . . . just some girl Jean-Georges was hitting on last night.'

If this isn't happiness, it feels exactly like it. We nibble *jamón Serrano* on the beach, the water is warm, Alice is tanned, which makes her eyes look green. In the afternoon we have a *siesta*. I lick the sea salt from her skin. We don't sleep much. While we're making love, Alice lists all the boys in Paris who have begged her to leave me for them. I tell her about the erotic dream I had last night. Why do the women I love always have cold feet?

Jean-Georges and Matilda join us for dinner. They seem besotted. They've just discovered both of them lost their fathers this year.

'But it's worse for me, because I'm a girl,' says Matilda.

'I hate girls who are in love with their fathers, especially when their fathers are dead,' says Jean-Georges.

'Girls who were never in love with their fathers either turn out frigid or lesbian,' I suggest helpfully.

Alice and Matilda dance together, looking for all the world like slightly incestuous sisters. We join them, dancing as a four-some. Everything seems perfect, things could have got out of hand, regretfully we go our separate ways, but we make up for it when we get to our rooms.

Just before I fall asleep, I finally do something radical: I take off my watch. If you want love to last forever, you need only live timelessly. It is the world we live in that destroys love. We should move here. Everything is cheap. I could fax stuff back to Paris, get a couple of advances from some publishers, send advertising campaigns by DHL . . .

And we would be bored to death.

\*

Dammit! I'm starting to panic again. I can feel the danger. I'm sick of being me. I wish someone would just tell me what I really want in life. It's true that sometimes our passion for each other begins to feel more like affection. Maybe the whole thing is starting again. I have to secrete more endorphins. I love Alice, and still I'm terrified we'll get tired of each other. Sometimes, we play at being boring on purpose. She'll say something like:

'Right . . . I'm off to do the shopping . . . See you later . . .'

And I'll say:

'And afterwards we'll go for a walk . . .'

'Pick rosemary . . .'

'Have a picnic on the beach . . .'

'Buy the papers . . .'

'Do nothing . . .'

'Or maybe kill ourselves . . .'

'The best way to die in Formentera is to fall off a bicycle, like Nico.'

I think if we can joke about it, maybe things aren't so bad.

The tension mounts. In four days, Alice and I will have been living together for three years.

# V

# D-Day −3

Though Alice and I make love less and less, it gets better and better. I stroke the few square inches of flesh she prefers. She closes my eyes. She used to have an orgasm every other time, now she comes every time. In the afternoons she leaves me to write and while I'm working, she lies on the beach in the sun. She comes back at about six and I make her an ice-cold Mauresque. Then I check her all-over tan. I squeeze her grape-fruits. She blows me then I fuck her up the arse. Afterwards, she reads over my shoulder as I write this and asks me to take out 'fuck her up the arse'. I agree, and write, 'I take her from behind' and as soon as she walks off, I press Command-Z on my Mac. This is the price you pay in fiction, the history of liter-ature is a litany of such betrayals; I hope she will forgive me.

I refuse to finish *Tender Is the Night*; I have a terrible sense of foreboding – things don't seem to be going too well for Dick Diver and Nicole. I listen to the 'Kreutzer' Sonata and think about Tolstoy's short story. The story of a man who murders his wife when he finds her with her lover. The couple were inspired by the violin and the piano in the Beethoven sonata. I listen as they sing together, interrupt each other, leave each other, find each other, flay each other and finally come together for the final crescendo. It is the music of a life lived together. The violin and the piano are incapable of playing solo ...

If our relationship suddenly falls apart, I don't care. I will never be able to give as much of myself to anyone ever again and I'll end my days fucking high-class whores and watching porn.

It has to work.

We have to get past the three-year mark. I change my mind every two seconds.

Maybe we should live apart. Living together is too exhausting.

I don't have any hang-ups, I'm not shocked by the idea of wife-swapping. After all, if you're going to commit adultery, you might as well do it together. An open relationship, maybe that's the answer: prearranged adultery.

No, I know: we need to have a baby, and fast!

I scare myself. The countdown marks off the Damocletian days. In three days, Alice and I will have been living together for three years.

# VI

# D-Day −2

Our mistake is in wanting life to stand still. We want time to stand still, love to last forever, nothing to die so that we can bask forever in some pampered childhood. We put up walls to protect ourselves, and one day those walls become our prison.

Now that Alice and I are living together, the only thing I put up are shelves. I treat every second I spend with her as a gift. I realise that sometimes, we can be wistful for the here and now. Sometimes, something wonderful will happen and I'll think, 'Wow. I will look back wistfully on this. I have to remember this moment so that I can think of it some day when things go wrong.' I realise that for love to last, a person must always have some mystery. We must avoid the hackneyed, not through feeble, fake attempts to surprise, but simply allow ourselves to be surprised by the miracle of the everyday. To be generous and honest. You know you are in love when you put toothpaste on a brush other than your own.

Most of all, I have learned that in order to be happy, you must first have been unhappy. Until you have learned to suffer, happiness will never be enduring. The love that lasts three years is the love that has not scaled mountains or lingered in the depths of despair, it is something that is handed to you on a plate. Love lasts only if everyone recognises its worth, and it is best to pay in advance or you may find yourself paying the bill afterwards. No one prepared us for happiness, because no one taught us the meaning of suffering. We grew up in a society in which comfort was a religion. You have to know who you are and who you love. You have to be a finished person to live an unfinished story.

I hope that the deceptive title of this book has not exasperated you too much: of course love doesn't last three years; I'm glad I was wrong. Just because something is published by Fourth Estate doesn't make it true.

I don't know what the past holds for me (as Sagan used to say), but I carry on, filled with wondrous dread, because I have no other choice; I carry on, less carefree than before, but I carry on just the same, I carry on in spite of everything, I carry on and it is beautiful.

We make love in the translucent waters of a deserted creek. We dance on the balcony. We flirt on the edge of a dimly-lit alley, drinking Marqués de Cáceres. We eat and eat. This is life. When I asked her to marry me, Alice's response was tender, romantic, beautiful, delicate, gentle and poetic:

'No.'

The day after tomorrow, we will have been living together for three years.

# VII

# D-Day −1

The sun is ineluctable. It may not be obvious, but I spent hours working on that sentence. The birds are twittering, this is how I know it is day. Even the birds are in love. This is the summer that The Fugees covered Roberta Flack's 'Killing Me Softly', and I know that I will always remember it.

'Marc, you know tomorrow is our third anniversary?'

'Shh! Shut up! Who cares? I don't want to know.'

'I think it's sweet. There's no need to be so horrible.'

'I'm not being horrible, I just need to get to work.'

'You know something? You're a selfish, pretentious bastard and you're so in love with yourself that it's sickening.'

'To be able to love someone else, you have to first love yourself.'

'Your problem is that you love yourself so much that there's no room for anyone else!'

She drove off on my moped, raising a magical line of dust along the dirt-track. I didn't go after her. When she came back a few hours later, I apologised and kissed her feet. I promised we would have a barbecue, just the two of us, to celebrate our anniversary. The flowers in the garden were yellow and red. I asked her:

'When are you going to leave me?'

'About ten kilos from now.'

'Hey, I can't help it if happiness makes people fat.'

At that very moment in Paris, an artist named Bruno Richard writes in his journal: 'Happiness is the silence of unhappiness.' Now he can die happy.

Tomorrow, Alice and I will have been living together for three years.

# VIII

# D-Day

Today is the last day of summer. On the beaches of Formentera, it's the last straw. Matilda has left without leaving a forwarding address. The wind whips through the low stone walls, through our feet. The sky is inexorable. Silence spreads across the Balearics.

Epicurus advises that serenity is achieved through simple pleasures of the present. Would love last longer if, instead of spending our time wondering how long it will last, we simply made the most of every moment? We will be friends. Friends who hold hands, who lie on the beach together snogging, who delicately fuck against the wall of a villa while listening to Al Green, but friends just the same.

A magnificent day crowns our anniversary. We went to the beach, swam and dozed, happy as sandboys. The Italian waiter at the kiosk on the beach recognised me:

'Hello, my friend Marc Marronnier.'

And I said:

'Marc Marronnier is dead. I killed kim. From now on, it's just me, and my name is Frédéric Beigbeder.'

He didn't hear a word with the music blaring. We shared a melon and some ice-cream. I put my watch back on. I had finally become myself, reconciled with space and time.

Evening came. After a quick detour to Kiosko Anselmo, where we had a Gin-Kas and listened to the wavelets slapping against the dock, we went back to the *casa*.

By starlight and candlelight, Alice was making a tomato and avocado salad. I lit a stick of incense. An old flamenco tune was playing over the crackle of the radio. The lamb chops were burning on the barbecue. The lizards were hiding under the *azulejos*. The crickets all suddenly fell silent. She sat next to me, smiling happily. We drank two bottles of rosé each. Three years. The countdown was over! What I had forgotten was that a countdown is always the beginning of something. At the end of the countdown, the rocket takes off. Hallelujah! And there I was fretting like an idiot!

The most wonderful thing about life is that it goes on. We kissed slowly, holding hands beneath the orange moon, listening to the future.

I looked at my watch: it was 11.59 p.m.